SHARING SECRETS, SHARING HER:

Uncovering My Girlfriend's Dirty Past Sparks a Kinky Femdom Getaway

By Lewis Crane

LEWIS CRANE

BLOG

https://lewiscraneerotica.blogspot.com/

EMAIL

lewiscranearotica@gmail.com

OTHER WORKS

Mistress Klein's Femdom Gym

Zenit

Sister's Pet

Three in a Barn

Snatch Competition

The Persia Rendezvous

I

When Emily and I first started dating, I knew my life had changed. But I had no idea just how wild things would get. Not until we took our first trip out of town. Everything changed the night we decided to take that vacation. Asheville in the fall. A cabin. The leaves on fire. A celebration of our new love. We decided to take that trip the same night we had that first fateful conversation about her past. The conversation that opened the door to our strange new world. And by the time we got home, my life would never be the same.

We'd only been dating for a few weeks when we first talked about going out of town together. We were laying in my bed. She was nestled in my lap, my fingers twisting in her hair. I felt so at peace.. I still couldn't believe I'd found a girl like Emily.

A couple years in the online dating wilderness had

jaded me. I'd nearly given up on the dating apps. So when I saw I'd matched with a slim blonde environmental scientist with a yoga body and a John Muir quote in her bio, I figured I was just being catfished again. But she ended up being very sweet and funny in our first text conversation. Before long we'd made our first date.

It was a relaxed coffee date. "No pressure," we agreed. "Let's just get to know each other." My first glimpse of her nearly knocked me off my chair. It was her face that struck me. She was even more gorgeous in person than she was in her pictures. Her shining smile was sweet, almost angelic, but there was a mischievous twinkle in her green eyes. Not a troublemaker's smile, really, but the smile of someone who wouldn't let rules get in the way of her fun.

I left our date still in shock it had even happened. It was a laid back date, to be sure- just coffee and a quick goodbye hug- but we had chemistry. I could feel it. I knew she could, too. I had that little feeling inside me, that flickering flame of hope that maybe things would be ok. Maybe this could work out. It had been so long since I'd felt that. I went to bed that night dreaming about seeing her again.

We continued seeing each other casually for the next few weeks. Between dates, we texted constantly. That's how I knew she was into me, too. I obsessed over keeping the jokes and the interesting conversations flowing without overwhelming her. To my surprise, I was killing it. She laughed at almost everything I said. She asked me probing questions about my life. She enthusiastically agreed to more dates. When we saw each other, our vibe was magical. And when at the end of a date to a wine bar I finally moved in for the good-night kiss, she caressed my cheek with her hand and held my mouth to hers for a long, lingering kiss that kept me up all night.

Despite our constant conversation, lots of her life remained a mystery to me. Especially her past relationships. I'd opened up to her about my last girlfriend- *god, had it really been 3 years?*- but when I pressed her about her own history, she evaded my questions. It was Trying to pin her down on the details was like trying to catch smoke. She'd just laugh and say, "nothing serious," or "I just never met the one," vague statements totally open to interpretation. But I didn't spend too much time worrying, though. It was better than other dates I'd been on, where girls went on and on about their exes. Mostly I was just overjoyed that she still seemed interested in spending time with me.

After a few low-pressure dates and lots of texting in between, I finally made my move. There was a performance of the Firebird that weekend at the local ballet company, and I knew she would be thrilled to go. She was a theater girl at heart- she'd even taken dance classes for years in high school. When I asked her to go with me, I could practically hear her squealing over text. Then I casually suggested we go out to dinner beforehand at Acropolis, one of the fanciest restaurants in the city. That was the move. That's what sealed the deal.

Our big date was a huge success. I felt like someone else was controlling my words and actions- I'd never felt so comfortable with someone before. We laughed our way through a bottle of wine and an Adriatic feast. I put my arm around her on the walk to the theatre. We held hands throughout the performance, and there were times I was so distracted by her beautiful face that I could hardly focus on the action onstage. Afterward, we headed to a bar for a nightcap and I summoned up the courage to ask her to come home with me. Our eyes met in the bar, hers glittering and warm, and she told me she would love to. We sealed our plan with a kiss in the bar.

We climbed into the Uber, both tipsy from our night of revelry, and once we closed the car doors we were all over each other. I felt bad for the driver, but not bad enough to keep my hands off Emily's waist as I kissed her lips over and over. By the time we got to my apartment we were dying for each other. We shed our clothes all the way from the doorway to my room as I led her to the bed. I couldn't believe the desire she brought out in me. I'd never been the most passionate guy in the world, but something about her sweet face and amazing body and the buildup of the past few weeks just made crazy for her. I threw her on the bed, and took a moment to marvel her smooth, perfect body laid out across the sheets. My cock was straining inside my briefs, and when I tugged them down it leapt into the air like it had a life of its own and pointed straight between her legs.

I climbed onto her, my hands feeling for her vulva, rubbing and caressing her slick warmth, my mouth on hers and on her throat and breasts, those perfect small ripe orbs. Her breathing came in gasps as I slipped my fingers into her, and her delicate hand reached up to wrap around my cock. "Please fuck me," she begged in my ear. "I want you so bad."

These words nearly drove me wild, and I took hold of my cock and plunged it deep inside her. She gasped as I entered, and pulled me up close to her. "Hold still," she whispered. "I want to feel you."

We lay together in the dark, my cock buried all the way in her to the hilt, feeling each other breathe and pulse in the dark. Slowly, she began to grind her cunt against me, squeezing my cock tight around the shaft. I held her tight and pushed against her, massaging her clit with the base of my cock. We worked our hips together like this, her breath hot and quickening in my ear, her fingers tracing over my shoulders.

I'd never fucked someone like this before. Usually I tried to emulate the porn stars I'd seen before and fuck them hard and fast with jackhammering strokes. More often than not, this just made me shoot my load embarrassingly early. But this time, held tight and deep inside her, her smooth thighs squeezing me tight against her, her eyes closed as she ground against me, I could savor the whole encompassing sweet feeling of her wet tight warm cunt grasping my cock and squeezing it.

Her breathing quickened, and I realized she was driving herself closer and closer to orgasm. It was all over her ragged breath and her quickening pace. Grinding. Thrusting. Driving her hits against mine over and over. All I could do was brace against her and let her work herself up, driving closer and closer into a crescendo until...

Suddenly she was moaning in my ear. It was the sexiest noise I'd ever heard. "I'm about to cum," she groaned, and suddenly a powerful orgasm wracked her entire body. I felt her cunt clench up against my cock, pulsating wildly as she came hard against me. This sensation and the wet warmth and the moans in my ear and the pure bliss of all this being somehow real was all too much for me, and with a groan I felt myself crossing the threshold.

"I'm coming too," I gasped.

"Cum inside me," she begged, her thighs twitching against me. "Fill me up."

And at that, I exploded deep inside her, just as her orgasm reached its peak, driving my cock deep inside her. She was so tight I could feel her cunt stretch as I twitched inside her, filling her up with a huge load.

I lay still inside her, our sweaty bodies entangled on the bed, the sweet damp smell of her hair in my nose as I caught my breath. Her fingers traced my shoulder blades.

All I could say was "wow."

Emily started giggling and squeezed me up against her. "I've been looking forward to that," she whispered in my ear. Her hot breath made me shiver.

I couldn't help but laugh too. "Me too," I told her. "And that was amazing. I've never… done it that way before."

Emily shrugged. Her smile was sweet, but her eyes had that strange mischievous glimmer to them. "It feels so good." She suddenly squeezed herself, tightening her pelvic floor. Her wet pussy contracted tight around my cock, squeezing it hard. It was growing softer in her, and the squeeze forced it out. My clock slithered out of her, and Emily gasped as a flood of my hot cum dribbled out of her.

I stared at her, her beautiful flushed face, her incredible tight lithe body, perfectly smooth, and the past few weeks' whirlwind romance swept through my mind. *Where did you come from?*

II

After that first magical night together, I felt like I was walking on air. I woke up cradling Emily against my chest, her golden hair cascading down to my stomach. She opened her eyes and smiled sweetly up at me. It was too early for mischief in her eyes; they simply shone with a happy, contented smile as she squeezed me gently.

"Good morning," she whispered. "I'm glad you're still here."

"You thought I'd sneak away?"

Emily shrugged, a brief shadow of sadness darkened her eyes. "You know how some guys are."

I cradled her close to me. "I've got news for you," I whispered. "You're gonna have to throw me out of here."

She giggled back and squeezed me again. Her hand lingered on my chest, then slowly she tiptoed her fingers down my stomach. Her fingers found my soft penis and closed around it. The mischief was in her eyes again.

The next thing I knew, she'd bent down and taken me in her mouth. "Oh my god," I groaned, the soft wet heat of her lips sliding down my cock. She started slow and tender, expertly teasing me with her tongue as my cock grew hard inside her mouth. Within seconds she'd worked me up to full staff, and I felt the tip of my prick start to press against the back of her throat.

It had been years since I'd gotten a blowjob. And never in my life had I gotten one this good. She sucked me deep into her mouth in long slow movements, her vacuum-sealed lips wrenching groans of pleasure from her. Her hand found my balls and rubbed them slowly, then pressed against the hard knot in my perineum at the base, forcing blood into my cock and stiffening me even further.

She had no problem with my fully-hard dick, sucking it down easily to the hilt. Her little muffled happy groans drove me wild. Up and down, up and down. Wet. Warmth. The sight of her sweet lips wrapped around my cock, taking me deep in her mouth. It gave me such a sense of power, and a sick and dirty thrill at watching such a beautiful girl pleasure me.

And what incredible pleasure it was, building up inside me, pulsing, warm and desperate until- "Oh, god," I groaned, "I'm about to-"

She stopped immediately. Slowly, she released her

mouth's grip around my dick, pulling back gingerly to make sure she didn't touch me. A hot tormenting pressure had built inside my cock that now twitched helplessly on my stomach. I reached for it, but Emily caught my hand by the wrist. Then she fixed me with a look of such playful innocence it almost made me cum hands-free.

"What do you think you're doing?" she smirked

"I," I stammered. "I was gonna-"

Emily laughed. "Don't be silly. I'm going to take care of that. In a minute." Suddenly she kicked the covers off and scooted up the bed. She spread her smooth thighs, revealing her perfect mound between her legs. "I want to have some fun, too," she said. "I hope you're not one of those guys who doesn't eat pussy."

Without a word, I flipped over and grasped her thighs with my hands. I might not have been the most experienced, but I'd never shied away from going down. And hers was the most delicious looking cunt I'd ever seen. Smooth pink lips parted slightly, glistening with a sheen of wetness, the sweet smell mixing with her sweat in an intoxicating blend.

I slid my tongue up her vulva, and she wriggled and writhed beneath my touch. Her fingers grasped my hair. I teased her open gently with long, slow licks up her pussylips. With one hand, I pinched her just around the clit from the outside and pulled, stretching her pussy open. Even through her lips I could feel how swollen her clit was.

I tried to tease her, but she was too horny. She pushed my head between her legs, and I dutifully kissed and licked around her entrance, feeling it stretch around my tongue. Gently I began to lick up toward her clit, my tongue just flicking around the outside.

"That's it," she breathed, her fingernails scratching my scalp. "Good boy."

Those words made my still-hard cock twitch again. I was so hungry for her I was tempted to jump up and slide my cock inside her. But I had a mission, and damn it I was going to make her happy. I continued lapping my tongue up and down her cunt with increasing pressure, judging how much pressure to use by her moans. When her breath caught tightly I eased off, making sure not to overstimulate her.

As I kissed around her clit, I pressed two fingers into her. Her cunt parted for them slowly, squeezing my fingers all along as I slid them in. It reminded me of how her spasming cunt had milked my cock the night before when she came, and drove me even crazier with hunger. I started finger-fucking her while I ate her cunt, bending my fingers up to rub her g-spot while stretching her open from the bottom.

"Oh, fuck yeah," she groaned, pressing her hips up to my face. I burrowed deeper, my lips rubbing her clit, my fingers crooked inside her. I slipped another inside and spread them. Her cunt stretched for my three fingers, and I slowly pumped them in and out of her while licking her harder.

"That's it, baby," she breathed. "Oh, god, you're going to make me cum!" I felt the orgasm build inside her to a peak. Then she gave a shuddering moan, and her thighs gripped my head. Her cunt spasmed wildly against my fingers as I drove deeper, pushing her through her ecstasy from inside and out. Her entire body twitched, her beautiful flat stomach taut and tight with the tension rocking through her body.

When the orgasm subsided, Emily caught her breath. "Wow," she gasped, smiling up at me. "That was pretty good."

I couldn't hide my pleasure at doing a good job. She laughed at my bashful smile and gave me one of her own. "Thank god you aren't one of those guys who doesn't go down," she said. "There are so many of them." *How many guys have-*

She broke my train of thought with a deliberate glance down at my still-stiff prick. She cocked an eyebrow. "I guess I'll take care of that now. You definitely earned it."

Before I could say a word, she leaned down and took me in her mouth. I was still on my knees in the bed, and her bent over body gave me an incredible view of the smooth curve down her back and up over her perfect round ass, to her thighs and her cute bare feet.

Emily arched her back seductively as she sucked me from all fours, her pretty green eyes fixed on mine. I ran my hands down the wave of her back and up to her butt, pushing her closer as she sucked my prick deep down her throat. I slapped her firm ass hard, hypnotized by its bounce. Emily gave a giggling moan and sucked me deeper. I was in such ecstasy, squeezing and kneading her ass, her beautiful eyes on me, my prick down her throat. I wanted it to last forever. But it ended up lasting about thirty seconds. I'd been so worked up by her before, and so turned on by the hot taste of her cunt, that I was poised to blow right when she started sucking me.

"Oh, god," I warned. "I'm about to cum." A brief smirk crossed her face before she redoubled her mouth's grip on my prick and took me all the way to the hilt. This hot enveloping grip was too much, and I lost control. Rope after rope of cum sprayed against the back of her throat. She kept her mouth locked tight around me, milking every drop out of me with her tongue and cheeks. I watched her throat pulse as she swallowed again and again, sucking down every drop.

When I finally finished, she pulled her head back and gasped for air with a big smile. "Damn!" she said, wiping at her mouth. "That was a huge load!"

"You're amazing," was all I could muster. She smiled again, then suddenly rose up and planted a kiss on my lips. It was wet and hot, and her saliva clung to my lips like dew. *I hope it's saliva*, I thought, but I didn't really mind as long as I was kissing her. I was completely, utterly smitten.

I still tasted her over our coffee that morning. Her sweet ripe scent clung to my nostrils even as I finally said goodbye and hugged her at the door. We kissed, again, long and slow and nearly fell down on the couch for another round. But I was late, the day was getting on, and so I left with promises for our next date.

I wandered throughout the day grinning like I'd just walked away from an insane asylum when the guards weren't looking. Tired, hungover, and overjoyed, the world was in soft fuzzy focus, and I practically danced through it like it was the movie set of my life. I couldn't believe the past day. The past weeks, even. And by the time I got home, she'd already texted asking me to come to dinner the next day. She'd cook.

III

And that's how it was for those first magical weeks. We couldn't keep our hands off each other. We texted and called and stayed up all night in bed, talking and loving and giggling and holding each other close in the dark. I went to work with fried braincells every day, that idiotic grin plastered under my bagging eyes. *Do I even need to sleep?*

I hadn't been this smitten since I was a teenager. And in my late twenties, after a barren stretch and the slog of online dating, I had stopped expecting to ever feel those kinds of butterflies again. But Emily inspired it in me. I had to laugh at my own sickly-sweet feelings schmaltz, reading poems to her in bed and slipping love-notes in her bag before work. She inspired the most romantic side of me. I couldn't have played it cool if I tried. There was no disguising the ardor I felt for her. The love she gave back made me feel safe to open up, safe to let her know how

20

special she was becoming to me.

And our sex life… I'd never experienced anything like it. I wasn't exactly a player in college, and the few flings and short relationships I'd had since then had been fun but lacked a kind of spark. I didn't know how much I was missing out until Emily. She brought out the animal in me. Everything about her inspired a primal lust; her sweet angelic face, that mischievous smirk, her lithe body and full ripe ass and slender waist and heavenly thick thighs. Even her cute feet and the scent under her arms could get me going. Her cunt was an altar to my new religion that I prayed to every time I could.

The only thing sexier than her body was her mind; and what a dirty mind it was. She blew me away constantly with her willingness to try things, experiment. Within days of our first encounter I was doing things I'd only seen in porn. She let me cum on her face. She begged me to let her taste her own sopping cunt from my fingers. She urged me to get rough with her, choke her air, pin her down, pull her hair. And she returned this roughness double, her nails slicing raw divots in my back, her teeth leaving bruises on my shoulders. I reveled in our passionate, wild love, and took every opportunity to enjoy her.

One morning while she was cooking breakfast, naked from our night before, I slipped up behind her at the stove and, without a word, bent her forward and thrust my cock in her. I fucked her in the mornings before work, and she'd keep me horny all day by texting me that she could still feel my cum dripping out of her during her staff meetings. I learned to fist her, pinning her down by her shoulders with her perfect ass in the air, working my hand deep inside her down to the knuckles until she was writhing like an exorcism.

One night I came home to find her laid out in lingerie on the bed; a tiny skirt with black fishnets and a front-clasp bra. She was displayed for me like a present. It was incredible how comfortable she looked with her own beauty, spread across the bed, knowing it would drive me wild. And it did. I was inside her before the skirt came off.

Much of her remained a mystery to me. Particularly her past. But during those love-drunk first weeks it never occurred to me to get too bogged down in her history. Even though she occasionally said things that hinted at a strange past.

Like when I brought up wanting to try anal sex with her- I'd fantasized about it since puberty, but had never been with a girl willing to give it a shot. But when I asked her, Emily smiled but looked away. "Typical guy," she laughed, but I caught something sad in her eye. "Well, maybe someday. But I've had too many guys just try to stick it up there."

How many is too many? I started to ask, but then lost my train of thought when her eyes met mine and that mischievous glow was back. "Maybe I'll have to fuck your butt first," she smirked. "So we can see how you like it."

I was so stunned by this suggestion, I forgot all about my other concerns. She was smiling, but there was an earnestness beneath her smirk that made me unsure if she was joking or not. But before I could ask a follow up, she pounced on me and play-humped me until I flipped her over, pinned her down, and fucked her again.

And it went on like this, those vague doubts and questions barely surfacing before being once again submerged beneath the all-consuming flood of love I felt toward her. Until, by accident, they bubbled up when we were planning our first trip.

It was getting on late fall, a crispness in the air, leaves just starting to turn, coffee and jeans and chilly mornings huddled under heavy blankets. We were reaching a level of comfort with each other, a familiarity as the rush of initial exploration subsided. We still burned for each other, but there was a sense of balance now. We could actually manage a good night's sleep every now and then. It was lovely.

One morning we were talking about our dread of the coming winter. She was laying back, her head nestled in my lap, my fingers toying in her hair. "Let's go somewhere," I said.

Emily idly patted my stomach. "Hungry, baby?"

"No," I said. "For the weekend."

Emily's eyes lit up. "A trip? That's awfully official," she teased.

I looked her right in the eye. "Yep."

Her eyes softened and she gave me that beautiful, heartbreaking smile. I leaned down and kissed her upside-down mouth. Her lips were soft and warm and perfect. I deepened our kiss, my sweet romantic feelings turning more lustful. My hands slipped up her slender body and cupped her small, firm breasts.

She giggled and pulled away. "You animal!" she cried with mock horror. "You just fucked me!"

"And I'm going to again," I said, my hands sliding down her stomach. My cock was beginning to swell up, pressing against her shoulders.

She slapped my hand away playfully. Our eyes met; hers were twinkling stars. She reached behind her and gave my stiffening cock a squeeze. "You can fuck me after we figure this out. Where do you want to go?"

"Asheville," I said, my hands creeping up to her breasts again. "We can get a cabin."

Emily smiled. "That's perfect."

"Great," I said, squeezing her perky nipples. Then I suddenly wrapped her in my arms and rolled her over on her back. "*Now* I'm going to fuck you again."

Emily squealed and struggled away from me. "Help!" she giggled, pulling her legs up defensively. "Not until we get a place booked. Bad boy."

And so we sat side by side in bed and browsed AirBnBs for a while on her phone, taking in several gorgeous options in the mountains. After a while, we found the perfect place: a rustic cabin with a big fireplace right next to a cozy-looking couch. We could just picture ourselves curled up together on that couch while a roaring fire crackled nearby, warming ourselves up with some spiked hot chocolate and each other's warmth. "That's the one."

While Emily booked the reservation, I tried to

make the moves on her again. She laughed me off. "Almost done!" She pulled up our confirmation email. It said the owner's name was Deirdre, and gave her email and phone number. Emily selected the phone number and saved it to her contacts. The pulled up the contact list and scrolled down until she found it. "There it is!" she announced, pointing to DEIRDRE AIRBNB.

But I wasn't looking at DEIRDRE AIRBNB. I was looking at the name right below it in her contacts. DERRICK D2B. That's all it said.

"Derrick D-2-B," I read. "Who's that, a protocol droid?"

Emily just laughed and tossed her phone aside. "Wow," she said. "That's a blast from the past."

"Yeah? A boyfriend?" I said, trying to sound teasing. But something in her reaction made my heart stick in my throat.

"Derrick?" Emily said. "Hell no."

I knew I was onto something. But I couldn't think of what to say. "What's D-2-B mean?"

Emily giggled and covered her eyes with her hands. "Oh, god," she said, embarrassed. "You don't want to know."

I wanted to stop asking, but I couldn't help myself. "Oh, I do want to know."

Emily fixed me with a little smirk. "Fine," she said. "It means 'Dick Too Bomb'."

My stomach churned. "What does that mean?"

Emily rolled her eyes. "He was one of those dudes who I knew was an asshole, so I didn't want to hang out with him. But…"

"Dick too bomb…" I murmured.

She shook her head. "Exactly. That's why he wasn't my boyfriend. He was such a douchebag. But he was great in the sack."

I was quiet. I thought of everything we'd shared. Her sexy moans, the way she pulled me into her, her yearning breathing on my neck. The sudden thought of someone else experiencing all that made me sick.

Emily sensed my awkwardness. "What's wrong?"

"Oh, nothing," I lied, wrapping her in my arms.

She squinted at me. "Come on. Spit it out."

"I don't know," I said. "It's just weird to think of you with someone else."

Her nostrils flared. Up to this point I'd barely seen her annoyed, but now I was starting to feel it. "You've fucked other girls."

"I know."

"Do you have a problem with the fact that I've had sex with other guys?" she pressed. Her voice was harder edged. "Do you wish I was a virgin?"

"No, it's not-"

"Because if I was a virgin," she went on, "I wouldn't know how to do all that stuff you love."

"I don't care-," I told her.

Emily looked away. "Just forget it," she said in a flat voice. Suddenly, she felt a thousand miles away from me.

"Hey, I'm sorry," I said. "I didn't mean to-"

"It's fine," Emily said in a tone that told me it wasn't. There was an awkward silence. I'd never felt this kind of tension between us before. She was lost in thought, her sharp teeth working on her lower lip. "There's a lot of stuff you don't know about me."

"Yeah?"

Emily kept going. "I've known a lot of guys like Derrick," she said. She bit her lip. "Truth is, I used to sleep around a lot."

"It doesn't-"

"Whatever you're thinking, it's probably worse," Emily went on. "I've slept with guys. Girls. One night stands. Threesomes. You name it."

My heart was pounding in my chest. Images jumbled in my mind of her naked body. The feelings we'd shared. And the sick thought of her with someone else. Suddenly everything came bubbling up. The off-handed comments she'd made about other guys. The weight of her body against me felt suffocating. I couldn't breathe..

Emily sighed again. "I've been here before," she said. "I start liking a guy, and then I open up about my past and they get freaked out. That's why I didn't talk about this stuff with you."

I silently rubbed her arms, trying to think of what to say. But Emily kept going. "But that's how it is. And if you have a problem with it, you should just tell me now."

I swallowed hard and looked down at her. Nothing as good as her had ever come into my life before. I had never been as happy as I felt when I was with her. So what if she'd had other guys before? Even lots of them? A secret doubt nagged at me, but I tried to push it away. *It doesn't matter*, I told myself. And then I told her. "It doesn't matter," I said. "I'm still crazy about you. I don't care about your past."

Emily flashed the sweet smile at me, her eyes twinkling. "Dang it. Why did I have to like you so much?" I leaned forward and kissed her lips, and before long I was parting her legs and sinking myself into her. But a part of me was distracted, and I knew that she could tell.

IV

The distraction lingered on even as we drove out to the cabin in the mountains. Our conversation was awkward and slightly strained. I was too enthusiastic, too eager to act like nothing bothered me. Emily was subdued, and eventually we settled into silence as I wove my car down the road.

It was a gorgeous drive out into the forest, as soon as we were off the interstate. The valley was lit up bright with the peak colors of fall, a radiant wall of orange and yellow that hemmed us in as I drove us up the mountainside. It was perfectly crisp out, the sun shining but the air cool.. Her hand was warm but stiff in mine, and my reassuring squeezes went unreturned. I looked over at her, lingering on her beautiful features, telling myself how lucky I was to be out here with her. Then suddenly the thought of someone else enjoying her, anyone else feeling the warmth between her legs and the cries in her voice and sharing kisses and secrets with her made me sick. *Guys. Girls. Threesomes. Had she really done all that before?* I looked away.

Emily felt that. "What are you thinking about?"

"Nothing," I lied.

She sighed and stared out the window. The silence resumed. I squeezed her hand again, but it was cold. "Just say it."

"Say what?"

She freed her hand with an irritated shake. "I can tell you're all bothered by our conversation."

"A little," I admitted.

"Why?"

I licked my lips. "It just makes me worry about making you happy. Knowing you had a lot of experiences before me. I get worried I won't be enough for you."

Emily looked at me like I was a little boy asking about the easter bunny. "Baby, there's more to life than sex," she said. She took my hand. Her sweetness was returning. "I like *you*. You're a great guy. That's all I care about right now."

I smiled back, but something still troubled me. "Did you really have threesomes?" I asked. "And sleep with girls, and all that?"

Emily snorted. "You really want to know about that?"

And that was the thing. Part of me *never* wanted to imagine her being close with someone else. I wanted to be the only one for her. I had to be the only one for her. But knowing there were others- *many* others- filled me with a sick curiosity, like the need to pull off a scab you'd know would ooze with blood. "Kind of," I admitted.

And so, as I weaved through the mountain roads on that gorgeous fall afternoon, heading on our first trip out together, she told me all about it. "I didn't start off wild," she told me. "I was a virgin until college, actually. But when I was growing up, I was obsessed with sex."

"Really?"

"Oh yeah," she laughed. "My parents were super conservative. They were completely anti-sex. I couldn't date, they wouldn't let me wear any cool clothes… it was such a drag."

"I didn't know they were like that."

"It was weirder, though," she went on. "They

literally always accused me of doing dirty stuff. They wouldn't let me be in my own room with the door closed."

"Why?"

"Why knows? They were both messed up. But, of course, it had the total opposite effect on me."

"Of course."

"I was obsessed with sex, and with hiding it. I used to look up 'sex' in the dictionary!" she laughed. "And get turned on! Can you believe that?" She shook her head. "I masturbated all the time. I was always afraid of getting caught, but somehow that fear of it just made me want to do it more. I read dirty stories on the internet, too- all the time."

"You did?"

Emily sighed. "Reading porn was my favorite thing. I could spend hours going down the rabbit hole. The dirtiest, nastiest, most perverted things. Stuff I'd never even heard of. I made it to eighteen without even kissing a boy, but I knew all about bondage, group sex, rape fantasies... it was crazy."

"So what happened?"

"By the time I got to college, I was practically dying for it. I couldn't wait to get away from my house. But it was weird," she explained. "I wanted to have sex so bad, but I was also so scared to. I was embarrassed about being a virgin. I think I came off way too strong," she told me. "Plus, my school was really small and conservative. People were constantly gossiping about each others' sex lives. The first thing the girls in my dorm told me was that I shouldn't sleep around. The whole thing built into this kind of crazy pressure I felt inside."

I didn't have to prod her anymore. I just kept my eyes on the road weaving between the changing leaves, allowing her the space to start talking. "I knew I was attractive, though. Lots of guys hit on me, or made compliments. But I would just get so awkward with them. I had no idea how to do dating or hookups in real life. Plus I was so scared of being labeled as a slut. So I turned to the internet."

"Online dating?"

"Kind of," she said. I could feel her embarrassment, and I reached over and pinched her reassuringly on her bare, smooth thigh. She went on. "I started... posting pictures of myself," she explained. "Dirty pictures. I hid my face, but... not much else."

"What were you doing in them?"

"There were lots of pictures of me in sexy outfits. Lingerie, schoolgirl clothes, animal costumes, you name it. Plus, tons of naked ones. And it wasn't just softcore. I would film myself getting off, fingering myself, fucking myself with dildoes and butt plugs. It was... a lot."

Images of her perfect lean body displayed naked for strangers on the internet suddenly sprang into my mind. I felt an involuntary twitch inside my pants that took me by surprise. "I got pretty well-known," she explained. "There were lots of hot girls baring their stuff on the internet, but they liked me because of the dirty stuff I did. But especially because of my imagination. I would take pictures with really dirty captions about the stuff I used to read about. Gang bangs and rough sex, that kind of thing. I started getting tons of comments."

I shifted in my seat, trying to hide my growing boner. Her dirty mind was always the biggest turn-on to me, and the thought of her indulging in these fantasies was starting to stir me. "Eventually, I started messaging with a guy from one of the forums. It turned out he lived in my city. He was older than me, and he made me feel really good. He complimented me a lot but was really respectful. Not pushy at all. Finally, I agreed to meet up with him."

I couldn't believe the effect this story was having on me. I started off the conversation so terrified by the ugly feeling in my gut, but there was something so intriguing and so arousing about the idea of this illicit correspondence. "Did you tell him you were a virgin?"

"Not until I got there," she said. "It was so scary. One night, I packed a bag of all my favorite toys and outfits and drove over to his place. I was terrified he was going to kill me the entire time," she laughed.

"Jesus, I bet," I told her. I pictured her, young and naive, driving to meet a stranger from the internet for sex with a bag of lingerie and toys. It was a scary thought. "How did you know you would be safe?"

"It was a crazy risk," she told me. "Looking back, it seemed so stupid. But it ended up being totally fine."

"Really?"

"Yeah." She paused. "Actually, it ended up a lot better than I thought."

My cock strained in my jeans, and I tried to keep my eyes on the road. My hand began to slip up her thigh slightly. Her skin was warm, responding to my touch, and her voice was faraway and throaty. Was she getting turned on? "Well, go on," I said, trying to laugh. "What happened?"

Emily giggled. "I was really surprised by him in person. He was a little older and fatter than in the pictures he sent me, but he was still cute, in a grownup kind of way. It's funny, he's probably the same age as I am now-thirty-something- but to me back then he seemed older than my dad," she laughed.

"He didn't even try to touch me when he opened the door. Which was smart, because if he'd tried to, I probably would have just turned around and run away. I was so scared." She swallowed. "I remember when he closed the door behind him, I started sweating. I was worried I was going to be trapped in there with him. His apartment was pretty small- a studio. It was clean, though, and it smelled good. Just like him."

"We sat at the table and he offered me a beer. I didn't know what to say. I'd never drank alcohol before." She started laughing again. "And that's how it all came out. I told him I'd never had beer. I'd never had sex. I'd never even kissed anyone before."

"What did he think about that?"

"He was shocked," she said. "He didn't believe me at first. After all the pictures I'd posted- I mean, they were… really dirty," she said, embarrassed. "I can't blame him. He must have thought I was a total nympho."

"I bet he thought it was hot that you were a virgin," I said, and I did, too. My cock was straining against my jeans.

"I know he did," she told me, and I was dying for her to tell me more. "But he didn't push it. We just sat there for a while drinking the beer and talking. I told him I'd been wanting to lose my virginity, but I was scared. And he just stood up and said, 'don't worry.' And started walking toward me. I felt frozen. My heart was beating so hard watching him walk over to me. I wanted to stop the whole thing and run away. But I couldn't move. And he leaned down and kissed me, right on the lips. I still remember how his lips tasted like that beer. He had foam in his beard."

"What happened next?"

"I was so stiff while he was kissing me at first. He was basically just pushing his mouth into my lips. But eventually I started kissing him back. And I let his tongue in my mouth, and I started shivering all over. I couldn't tell if I was getting turned on or about to have a panic attack. But he knew I was nervous. And he just whispered in my ear that it was ok, that he was going to take care of me. And the next thing I knew he was walking me over to the bed."

"He lay me down with our clothes still on and I could feel his dick through his pants, pushing up between my legs. I felt like my whole body was on fire. But he treated me perfectly. So gentle, but so firm and confident. He took off my clothes and kissed me all over my body. His hands were so strong on my arms. He whispered to me about how I was beautiful. His mouth on my neck and his teeth on my ears almost made me faint. I was so scared and so worked up."

"I kept telling myself that I would stop him soon. At least so we could take a break. But he kept going, and I let him. He took off my pants and he pressed his palm up against my panties and I remember shivering all over. That's when I knew I was turned on. And all of a sudden the fear started going away and I realized how badly I wanted him."

"But he didn't fuck me at first, not right away. I

remember he spent a long time between my legs with my panties still on, just playing with my pussy though them. Licking it. Smelling it a lot. He said I smelled so good. I couldn't believe it. I could barely even think. I was so sensitive."

"Suddenly I wanted to feel his dick. It just came over me all of a sudden. I'd never seen one in person before, and the desire just came over me so strongly that I remember pulling away from him. He must have thought I was trying to stop him. I told him I wanted to see his dick, and he laughed. He must have been relieved."

"He stood up off the bed and pulled his pants down. He let his dick catch in the waistband of his underwear so that it popped out like a spring. It scared me how it jumped up like that, and how it pointed straight at me. I was almost too scared to touch it. But he took my hand and guided it over to him. Wrapped my fingers around it. And I started rubbing it. I had no idea what I was doing, of course, but I'd read enough porny stories to get the point."

"It seemed so big to me, although by now I know

he was pretty average. Thank god," she laughed. "I remember how strange it felt in my hand. And then he told me to put my mouth on it. I was so shocked, but I did it. He held me by the back of the head but he didn't shove my head down. Another thing to thank him for- I probably never would have given a blowjob again if he'd done that. But he just held me firm and let me start kissing and licking around his head.

"I remember thinking I'd be amazing at blowjobs- I'd posted enough videos of me sucking on dildos-" *the sudden image in my mind of a dildo slid down her throat on camera, my cock twitching-* "but the real thing was so different. I think he was enjoying it, but I really didn't know. I remember feeling confused. And then feeling really embarrassed. Sucking a stranger's dick, when just a few minutes before I'd never even been kissed... what would my parents say? I felt like such a slut."

"I think he could tell I was feeling bad, and he stopped me. He lay back on the bed and put his arms around me and asked if I was feeling ok. I told him I just needed a break, and we lay there in the bed for a minute while he held me close and kissed the back of my head. I was still shivering in his arms. And his penis was still sticking up, so hard. It was all so strange, I just wanted to leave. But I kept laying there, feeling his arms on me, breathing so hard."

"We lay there for a while, talking. I told him I couldn't believe what we were doing. That I was embarrassed to be so new to everything, and that I felt really awkward. He was so sweet about it. He said I was doing fine, and that I didn't have to worry about anything. He kept rubbing my arms and my back and eventually the feelings started to go away, and he was kissing me and I kissed him back and suddenly I was feeling his cock again. It was still hard and I was just like, I'm doing this. And I told him I wanted it."

"He didn't say anything. He just pulled my panties off and got between my legs. I'll never forget how he looked sitting on his knees between my legs, stroking his hard cock. I'd never felt so scared and vulnerable in my life. He was a big man- everything about him just seemed so big and old and strong- and I was laying there with my legs open, totally naked. I was so scared."

"Then suddenly he was rubbing his dick head against my pussy. It felt hot as lava. He was pushing, teasing, stretching me just a little bit, up and down. Touching my clit and then rubbing down to the hole, then teasing open the hole just a bit. I kept waiting for him to shove it in, and I was so scared he would, but he just kept rubbing it on the outside until I realized that I was dying for him to put it in me."

"And that's when he pushed it inside," she said.

"Did it hurt?"

"So bad," she told me. "But in a strange way. It was just such a intense stretching pressure pushing me open. Like I was getting impaled. But nothing ripped. Nothing tore. It was just this slow, relentless pushing open of me, deeper and deeper. I kept thinking he had to be done and somehow there was just more dick, pushing me open, deeper inside me. Until finally he pushed his hips to mine and I felt the tickle of his pubes and I knew he had filled me all the way up."

"I just lay there for a while, totally stunned. It was

like I'd been stabbed, and was trying to figure out how bad it was. We just breathed there together on the bed while my pussy pulsed around his dick. It was so sore and throbbing. But when the soreness started to go away, the throbbing kept going. And when he started to pull his dick back out of me, the whole feeling started all over again and I could swear that he was going to tear me in half."

"And then he put his lips up to my ear and his breath on my ear was hot just like his cock inside me was hot, and his whiskers tickled me and he growled in my ear. He said 'you're not a virgin anymore', and I didn't know if I was happy or sad but I knew I felt like I might cry.

"And suddenly he was fucking me. Pulling it out and pushing it in, slow but hard. His hips were pushing up into mine and I could feel his hipbone pushing on my clit. It was such a shock to me how good it started feeling. The pressure of his body on me, and his strong arms around me. The feeling of my pussy opening up for him. How each stroke seemed smoother and wetter until I could *hear* myself sucking him up inside me."

"Jesus christ," I groaned. My hand had slipped higher up her thigh, teasing around the bottom of her shorts. She must have known she was turning me on. She didn't say anything; she just took my hand in hers and slid it down her shorts. Her pussy was on fire when my fingers touched it, wet and warm, panties soaking with her juices.

Emily closed her eyes and leaned back in the seat as I started rubbing her pussy while she talked. "He kept going, faster and faster, and I was going crazy. My whole body felt like it was on fire. And he was whispering in my ear, telling me how good I felt, that I was all his, that I was his good girl. And I just wanted him to take me. I didn't even think about cumming; all I wanted was for him to fuck me and use me and make me his and to give myself completely over to him."

I was slipping my fingers inside her now, stretching open her swollen cunt while she talked. She ground her hips against me, pressing urgently against my hand. I looked over at her face; her eyes were closed, and her pale cheeks were flushed beet red. She continued, talking in a low voice.

"His back started sweating and his groans got deeper and I realized he must be getting close. He told me he was going to cum, and I still can't believe this but I told him, yes, cum, please cum inside me. I was begging him for it. I could feel how hard his dick was inside me, so hot and hard and throbbing so much as he got closer and closer and fucked me hard. It was sliding in so easy, pushing me apart over and over even though it felt like it had grown twice as big inside me."

I slipped a third finger in her, opening her wider while my palm pressed firmly against her clit. She bucked against me, working herself up against my hand as she talked.

"Suddenly he just slammed it deep into me and pressed it there," she said. I could feel convulse against me in my hand. "I could feel everything," she told me. "I could feel him twitch and I felt that hot thick flood of wet that mixed with my wetness and all I could do was pull him close and wrap my legs around him. I wanted all of it, every drop, as deep inside me as I could take it. I wanted him to cum forever, just shoot inside me again and again and again," and with every *again* she ground herself harder against me.

She lost control of her words at this point. Eyes pinched, both hands clasped around my wrist, she ground herself into my hand as my fingers pushed deeper inside her. I could feel her orgasm building. The sight of her pretty face contorted with pleasure was unbearable. I didn't even care that she was driving herself to orgasm by her memory of fucking someone, *fucking, no, not fucking, gettting fucked, getting fucked hard and good for the first time, getting taken and spread open and fucked and filled to the brim* and suddenly her orgasm reached its peak and she was writhing against me, moaning as the pleasure rippled through her body in the car seat.

When the last waves finally subsided, she was left panting for air. "Oh, man," she breathed, blowing a damp strand of hair from her lips. Her face was flushed beet red, and that mischievous smile was playing on her lips again. "That was surprising."

I gently slipped my fingers out of her, feeling her cunt slip over my knuckles and release them bit by bit. She gasped as I pulled away from her. Then, with a dirty wink of my own, I put my fingers to my nose and inhaled her richness. "He was right about your pussy," I told her. I tasted her clinging wetness from my fingers. "It's the sexiest scent in the world."

"Dirty boy," she laughed. "Did hearing about that really turn you on?"

The outline of my rock-hard cock straining against my jeans answered for me. I indicated it with my eyes, and she covered her mouth in mock-horror. "Look at that!" she said. She reached out cautiously, like she was trying to pet a sleeping tiger, and prodded my dick gently. Then she shrieked playfully and pulled her hand back. "Pervert," she teased. "I can't believe that story turned you on so much."

"Me either," I said. It hadn't really hit me yet just how strange it was to get so turned on by my girlfriend's story about getting fucked. I was just too horny to care. It *was* hot, imagining her so innocent and naive, how it felt for her to get fucked for the first time, picturing her splayed out on that bed with her legs spread and a flow of cum dripping out of her.

I didn't even realize I was rubbing my cock until Emily slapped at my hands. "Hey, wild boy," she scolded. "Keep your eyes on the road! You'll kill us out here!"

She was right- the road was winding and unfamiliar, and evening was starting to set in. But I was so worked up I thought I might explode, and I told her that. "Not fair," I said. "You got to cum."

Emily shrugged. "Sorry about your luck," she said. "Don't worry, I'll take care of you when we get to the cabin. How long until we get there?"

I glanced at the GPS. "Half an hour."

Her eyes had that mischievous twinkle that let me know she was playing with something in her mind. "Well, then. I guess I have time to tell you a couple more stories until we get there.

V

Emily kept me hard as a rock for the rest of drive as she told me the rest of the story about losing her virginity. The sweet teasing voice and her occasional touches of my painful stiff prick had me so horny I couldn't even think about how strange it was that her story about fucking someone else got me so turned on. I couldn't even think, period. I was just consumed by my hunger for her, by the pressure building up inside me that she delighted in making worse and worse as we drove.

They had sex again that same night. "A bunch of times," she told me, tickling her fingers against my cock as I struggled to keep my eyes on the road. "Even though I was so sore from the first one. He totally took his time with me. It ended up being amazing."

She told me how she tried on the lingerie she brought with her, microskirt and black fishnets with the front clasp bra. "Wait a minute," I broke in. "Is that the same-"

Emily giggled. "The night I laid out on the bed for you? That's the one."

I swallowed hard. I could still picture how she looked laid out in that incredible lingerie, displaying herself for me. The lace and ribbons like a present. I never thought she bought it for me- I wasn't thinking much about anything other than ripping off her panties and sinking inside her. I never considered that she'd worn it for someone else before. But now I saw her in that lingerie on the night she told me about, ashamed and happy and proud and scared, displaying that beautiful perfect body for someone else. Another man who must have felt that same animal hunger she inspired in me, feasting his eyes on her body and taking her in his hands, and her letting him, wanting him-

She brushed my cock again. It pulsed like an artery, filling me with warmth. "Did you really think I'd never worn that for anyone else?" she asked.

"Keep talking," I murmured. "What happened next?" My hand subconsciously ran down beneath my waist to squeeze my twitching cock. She slapped it away sharply, startling me.

"Bad boy," she scolded. "Keep that up and I might not let you cum at all."

"I can't help it," I whispered. "I'm so turned on."

"Well, you're going to love this next part, then," she said. She told me how he made her suck him again. How he pushed his cock into her mouth, and told her how to do it right. How it felt to feel him growing in her mouth. How she could taste his cum and her own cunt on his cock as it stretched inside her mouth. How it choked her, and how she liked it. And how he finally came inside her mouth.

"He told me to swallow it all," she said, "and I just nodded. Then he held me down in place. I couldn't believe how much came out. He had just filled me up so much inside my pussy. But it was huge. I was struggling but he just held my head still. I couldn't look away from him. He told me I was a good girl, over and over, like this." Her fingers fluttered over to my cock. "Good girl," she cooed, tickling me. I shivered. "Good girl. Good girl."

She must have known that I was getting

dangerously close to the edge, because she backed off for a while after that. But the stories continued, with her malicious giggles, as she told me how he made her ride him. She was sore and took her time sliding down and he stayed rock hard as she twitched and jerked on top of him, opening up to accommodate his swollen cock. "I didn't know how lucky I was at the time," she giggled. "Now that I've slept around some more, I can't believe how hard he got. And stayed. He must have cum four or five times!"

"He must have been so turned on by you," I said. She knew I was right. He couldn't keep his hands off this incredible, innocent virgin who had turned up at his apartment to give herself to him. He must have thought he was in heaven. The lucky bastard. I heard all about how he made her show him how she played with the toys she brought. How he coaxed her into slipping one of her plugs inside her virgin ass. And how at the last, he bent her down on all fours and railed her. This one was for him. He wasn't trying to ease her into it anymore. He gripped her hips and slammed himself into her, over and over, spearing her with his insatiable cock. He spanked her ass, and jerked her back by the hair. His fingers closed around her throat. And he growled in her ear that she was just a little slut.

"I loved that," she said, and I could tell she was starting to get turned on again by the story. Her fingers were toying with the fringes of her shorts again. "All my life I was terrified of being a slut. And something about him saying it in my ear, *growling* it like that while he fucked me… I felt like a slut. And I loved it."

She leaned back against the seat shrugged. "That's pretty much it," she smiled. That flush was playing around her cheeks again. "I hung around a little longer, but I had to get back to school. I just picked up my stuff and took off."

"Did you ever see him again?"

"Yeah, a few times," she said. "But he got weird on me. He was always in his own head about it. Either wanting me to be his girlfriend, or feeling like he should break the whole thing off. He felt guilty about the age difference. He was embarrassed to introduce me to his friends."

"What did you think about it?"

Emily laughed. "I didn't give a shit," she said. It was startling to hear her talk that way. "I didn't want to be his girlfriend. I had college, and friends, and a life. I was fine with going over there every week or so. He never seemed to understand that."

"Did you break it off?"

"It just kind of fizzled," she explained. "I got tired of him making drama where there didn't need to be. Besides,' she said, and she touched me on the thigh teasingly again. "I found some other outlets."

I swallowed. "Yeah? Other guys?"

But just then, Emily jabbed her finger out the passenger window excitedly. "That's it!" she squealed

And there it was- the cabin. Our home for the weekend. A clean and happy A-frame, mossy shingles stretching all the way to the ground, secluded under boughs of yellow birch. The timbers were new and practically polished, and a wide deck stretched out to greet us. Stretching fingers of the evening twilight reflected off the floor-to-ceiling windows and turned them into streaks of fire. It felt like coming come.

I crunched my car up the gravel drive and stopped it near the door. The clean birch scent filled our lungs like a first breath when we climbed out of the stuffy car, with pins and needles running through our thighs and calves as we struggled off the driving. My cock still pressed against the side of my jeans, no longer stiff but still full and hanging heavily.

Emily was overjoyed. She ran right up to the cabin door without grabbing anything and punched in the code. Then she threw the door wide. "We're here!" she exclaimed, as if announcing our arrival to whatever critters could be hidden inside.

I loaded myself down like a pack mule with our bags and struggled up the stairs. Emily ran to the car for a load of her own, darting past me like a forest sprite. It took only a few trips for us to bring our things inside and make a big pile in the foyer.

Then we looked around the cabin. It was rustic and simple, with high ceilings etched with wooden beams. The layout was small: one main room, with a big couch and a stack of blankets facing a wood stove. A kitchen with outdated orange countertops and a dingy one-pot coffee maker. And bathroom and bedroom tucked away to the side. But opposite the front door was a massive wooden deck, stretching out over the hillside. It offered an incredible view of the expanse of glowing mountain forests spreading out before our eyes.

I was about to say something, but Emily suddenly shivered. "It's cold in here," she said, and I couldn't blame her. The athletic shorts and t-shirt she was wearing when we left were no good up there in the mountain chill.

"Go change," I told her. "I'll make a fire."

"Ooh," she whistled approvingly. "Man make fire. I love it." She took her bag and headed to the bedroom, then closed the door behind her.

I sat in front of the big iron stovepipe on the floor-

scraps of wood and tinder were neatly piled up nearby- and started building a teepee inside. Before long, I had a little crackling blaze going. I babied it constantly with steady, shallow breaths of air. Bit by bit I build the fire up, snapping twigs and sticks until the warmth crackled against my face. There is something primal in the concentration of nursing a fire from spark to blaze, a place the mind goes where thoughts cannot follow. It is a meditative experience. Watching the flames lick up every twig and leaf, the direction of the smoke, deciding when to feed and when to watch..

I was so caught up in this firebuilding trance I didn't even notice Emily leave the bedroom until she was right behind me. "Looking good!" Her words startled me. I turned around. The sight dropped my jaw.

She wore an open flannel shirt that framed her taut stomach and teased the ripeness of her hidden breasts. A pair of long fuzzy socks were pulled up over her knees, slightly pinching the full flesh of her thighs. Her golden hair was tucked beneath a yellow knitted beanie pushed back to the top of her forehead. The only other thing she wore was simple pair of white cotton panties that peeked out between the shirttails dangled beside her hips. She stood there, casually displaying herself to me with the full knowledge of how good she looked, every line on her firm body licked by fingers of firelight that made her pale skin glow.

I saw she was waiting for a response from me, and I tried to pick my jaw up off the floor and think of something clever. "I thought you said you were cold."

Emily gave an embarrassed giggle and pulled up on her fuzzy socks. "These are really warm," she told me. "Besides, the fire's coming along great!"

She flounced onto the couch with a sigh, and drew her thighs up to her waist. I fed another log into the stove, trying to keep my cool when all I could think about was taking her. I watched the fresh log until the first tendrils of smoke began to rise. And then I was up and moving toward Emily. She opened her arms toward me, and pulled me close to her against the couch. I'd been planning to jump her bones right away, but something in the way she squeezed me tight stopped me. I just nestled into her, wrapping my arms under hers and savoring the feeling of my cheek against her bare chest as she stroked my hair.

"This is so nice," she murmured, her fingers tangling in my hair. "I'm so happy to be here with you."

I responded with a tight squeeze, and then looked into her eyes for a kiss. She bent down and softly pressed her lips to mine. When she pulled back, her eyes were shining with that familiar mischief. "So, what do you want to do now?"

With her dressed in that outfit, after the unbearable horniness she build in me during the drive, there was only one thing on my mind. I slipped my hands beneath the flannel and cupped her bare back up to me. My mouth was in her neck and ear. "I want to fuck you."

She nuzzled into me, cupping my mouth between her cheek and shoulder my mouth and teeth on her. Down below, her hand gripped my stiffening cock through my jeans. "Oh, my goodness," she said. "You're so hard."

"You got me so horny driving up here," I told her. "I feel like I"m already on the edge."

She scooted back a little to slow things down, but kept her hand resting lightly on my cock. Her eyes were shining inches from mine. "That's so wild," she said. "How do you feel about that?"

"About what?" I asked, reaching for her wrist.

"Getting so turned on listening to me tell those stories."

I was kneeling between her legs, one hand pressing hers against my cock, the other stroking her thighs just above the top of the overknee socks. I could barely think straight. "I mean, it's weird. I get that. But there was something so hot about listening to you. You were so turned on."

"Why do you think it turned you on so much?"

I shook my head and smiled down at her. "Emily," I said. "You are the sexiest girl I've ever laid eyes on. Everything about you drives me crazy."

"You're sweet," she giggled.

"I'm serious. I just can't get enough of you," I said. "I mean, look at you," I said, gesturing to her body. She must have known how incredible she looked in that open flannel and overknee socks and beanie and the simple cotton panties, laying back on that couch on display for me. "You're like all my fantasies came true. And something about those stories, and knowing about the dirty side of you and how turned on you were getting while talking to me, just made me crazy."

She sat back against the couch, pulling fully away from me. "Take your pants off," she ordered.

I obeyed at once, standing off the couch and unbuckling my jeans. My cock was standing out rock hard against my boxer-briefs when I dropped my pants. "Those, too," she said. I slipped my underwear down, straining my dick against the waistband until it popped out and bobbed in the air.

"Good boy," she said. She stood up and drew close to me, her lips near mine. I thought she was reaching for my cock, or leaning in for a kiss, but she just took my shirt by the hem and pulled it over my head. Suddenly I was fully naked in the cabin, my dick still standing straight out. I wanted to kiss her, but she was moving around me, *gliding* around in a circle with her eyes locked on mine until she was behind me. Her hands found my wrists and pulled them back behind me. And the next thing I knew, she was tying my wrists together with the t-shirt she'd just stripped off from me.

"I like where this is going," I said, allowing her to bind me up.

"Shh," she whispered softly. She gave the t-shirt binding a firm tug tight, tying my hands behind my back. And then she circled back in front of me, her face alive with mischief. She was staring me up and down with an appraising smirk, shamelessly running her eyes up and down my naked body. I felt so vulnerable under her gaze. She leaned forward, bringing her lips within an inch of mine. I closed my eyes and leaned forward to meet her kiss. But instead she pushed me hard on both shoulders. I tried to raise my hands to catch my balance, but they caught in the t-shirt and I wobbled backward and fell down on the couch.

From my seat on the couch the view of Emily standing in front of me was mesmeric. She was an ethereal forest spirit, the firelight behind her turning the golden curls of hair escaping from her beanie into translucent filaments of light. The shadows teased her lean body under the unbuttoned flannel, the long line of flesh from her navel to her throat glowing with the first flush of sweat. That smirk, that mischievous smirk was all over her face as she looked down at me, naked and helpless on the couch, my stiff prick throbbing beyond the reach of my bound hands.

"You're such a dirty boy." Her voice took on a low, bewitching tone as she slipped deeper into her character. She reached out a leg, delicately balancing on one foot, and pushed the other sock-covered foot against my painfully hard cock. It twitched violently, the veins standing out in full relief against the firelight. She was balanced like a ballet dancer, one foot prodding my aching cock, sliding up and down to the base and kneading my balls. "I can feel all that cum inside you already."

"I want you so bad," I moaned, struggling with my hands.

She silenced me with a finger to my lips. "I know you do, baby," she told me. "But where's the fun in that? You've been working up this nice big load for me all day. If I made you cum right now, don't you think it would be… anti-climactic?"

"I'm pretty sure it wouldn't take long to work up another," I told her. "I already feel like I could cum fifty times for you tonight."

Emily giggled and put her hands over her mouth, the mask of control slipping just a minute. "Oh my god," she laughed. Then she composed herself, standing taller, eyes narrowed, assuming a cold, appraising quality. "Well, as much as I would like to see your fifty loads some night, I'm going to make you wait for this one."

She smiled down on me, her fingers tracing the hanging shirttails of her flannel. "You like what you see?"

"I love it," I groaned. "You look incredible."

"The socks, too?" she asked. She bent slightly at the waist, thrusting out her perfect peach butt to tug the wooly socks a little higher up her creamy thighs. My senses swam.

"You're the sexiest thing I've ever seen in my life," I told her.

She giggled again, and ruffled my hair with her fingers. "Sweet boy," she said. Then she looked down at the simple cotton panties that strained against her thighs and ass. "What about these? They aren't very exciting."

"No, they-"

She shushed me again. "You want to know what's special about these panties?"

I nodded, my eyes locked on her with rapture. She ran her fingers through the waistband. "These were the same ones I was wearing in the car. You got them so dirty before when you were fingering me. I think they're still wet."

"Oh, god," I groaned.

"I was wearing them all day," she went on. "And now they're getting all sweaty with me standing by the fireplace." They were darker where they strained around her mound, and I could see where her vulva split through them. She slipped her hand past the waistband, and I could see her fingers sliding up against her through the underwear. Her eyes fluttered when the fingers slipped inside, and a little smirk crossed her face. Then she pulled her fingers out and held them deliberately to my nose.

I inhaled the scent from her glistening fingers, savoring the hot richness of her cunt. "See how turned on you got me," she said, watching me smell her. Then she pushed her fingers into my lips. I opened my mouth and let her feed me, sucking her slick juices greedily from her fingers. "Good boy," she breathed, watching me.

She pushed her fingers deeper into my mouth, and I swallowed hard as they pushed against the back of my throat. Then she slowly slid them out, leaving a thin trail of saliva that stretched then dribbled down my chin.

71

"Looks like I'm not the only one who was turned on."

My prick answered for me, throbbing helplessly in my waist. She batted her eyelashes at me with sweet false innocence. "You want me to take care of that, baby?"

"Yes," I moaned. "Please, I want it so bad."

"Aw, poor baby." She slid down beside me on the couch, and her warm body settling into mine felt like stepping into a hot shower. She reached out and teasingly touched the tip of my prick with her finger, making it jump again.

"Please," I begged her.

She took my cock in her hand and squeezed it hard around the shaft like she was appraising a cucumber at the store. "You're so hard," she said. Our eyes locked, and I was consumed by her mischievous little smirk and her shining eyes that promised new depths of pleasurable suffering. "You really must have liked my stories."

I tugged uselessly at the t-shirt tied behind my

back and tried to thrust my hips up to make her jerk my cock. She just squeezed harder. "You liked it, didn't you?" she repeated with another firm squeeze.

"I did," I gasped.

Squeeze. "You liked hearing stories about what a little slut your girlfriend used to be?"

"Yes."

Squeeze. "You liked hearing about how I got fucked for the first time?" *Squeeze.* "How I spread my legs for a stranger and let him take my virginity?" *Squeeze.* "Do you wish that was you?" *Squeeze.* "Did it make you jealous?" *Squeeze.* "Do you want to hear more?"

And yes, yes, yes, is all I could repeat, every time she squeezed my prick it was like she squeezed the word out of me. I was begging for more, begging for her hands on me, so desperate to feel the release that had been building inside me since the drive. And she knew it, and she was reveling in her control over me.

"You like my slutty stories, don't you, dirty boy?" she cooed in my ear, and it sent a shiver down my spine. "You want to know about all the dirty things I've done?"

And suddenly she was on top of me, thighs straddling my leg, her face buried in my neck. The heat at the center of her thighs under her panties burned against my desperate prick, and the heat of her tongue and teeth on my ear nearly convulsed me. She rocked her hips back and forth, teasing my dripping cockhead with the damp straining panties.

"Tell me," I begged her, my bound hands thrashing helplessly behind my back.

"Oh, dirty pervert," she whispered breathlessly in my ear as she rode against my cock. She seized my earlobe in her teeth. Her fingers clawed my throat. "Getting so turned on hearing about what a slutty girlfriend you have. Can you picture me, getting my sweet pussy spread open by another man? Knowing how many times I've gotten pumped full of cum? How I've sucked and swallowed and licked and eaten and been tied and fucked and spanked and slapped and choked and railed raw and hard until I was screaming?"

She bucked her hips in a wild rhythm against me, harder and harder like a frenzied dance. "Your girlfriend is a dirty whore," she growled in my ear. "And you love it, don't you?"

I was convulsing from the unbearable pressure that had built inside me, dying for the release. "I love it," I cried into her hair. "Please, let me cum."

"Don't you dare," she hissed, squeezing me tighter. She reached down and gripped my prick hard in her fist. "Don't you dare cum, you dirty boy."

I pinched my eyes shut, desperately trying to stop the buildup inside me. My entire body twitched from the exertion. Even as she slowed down, the feeling of her swollen cunt through her panties pressing against my dick had me right on the edge. "You don't get to cum until I say," she said. She reared back; her eyes were ravenous. She clapped a hand against my mouth, squeezing my lips hard and pressing my head to the back of the couch. With the other, she released my prick and slid it inside her panties. I could feel her fingers slip inside her cunt, her knuckles arching through the fabric against my prick.

She held me pinned against the couch with her hands mashing my face, eyes an inch from mine as she feverishly fingered herself. "I'm so fucking wet," she told me. "Taste it." And then those fingers were in my mouth, pushing past my lips and I was sucking, licking, tasting, breathing in the heavenly scent she smeared across my lips and tongue.

And then her hand was darting back inside the panties, inside her cunt. I could feel she had at least three fingers thrust inside her, working them deep against the third knuckle, stretching herself wide and rubbing her clit against her fingerpads. And then her lips were on mine, her tongue slipping into my mouth as she held my face still and kissed me deep and hard, swirling the juices she had just fed me as she held my face tight and drove herself closer.

I felt her orgasm build, sensed it from the first shuddering breath she drew that let me know she was getting close. Her knuckles teased against my cock, barely brushing it as she burrowed inside her cunt. She pulled her lips from mine and our eyes locked. Her mouth contorted in wordless gasps as the pressure built and her fingers worked deeper and faster inside. And then the shadow passed over her eyes and I knew that she was gone, lost on the wave that was just beginning to crash over and consume her. From deep inside her, a shaking low moan rattled out of her. Her thighs were crushing against mine, seizing and squeezing them tight as the pleasure washed over her.

The sight of her in this ecstasy, her ragged shuddering moans, the warmth of her pressed against me, the taste of her on my lips, the visions she had implanted in my mind, were all too much to bear. Even the sensation of her knuckles just barely brushing my stiff cock through her panties was too much for me. I was losing control. "Oh, god," I groaned in her ear. "I think I'm going to-"

And she just continued coming as she stared into my eyes, panting gasps of hot breath into my face as she rode the wave of pleasure, and just like that I was coming too. My stiff prick bucked in the air and started shooting a fountain, a *geyser* of all the cum she had worked up in me all day, the load I had been so desperately needing to release for hours now. It squirted into the air, rope after rope that splattered against our stomachs. I'd never felt the sensation of coming without something actually on my prick, but once that delicate brushing of her knuckles took me to the edge I did not stop until my cock had fired half a dozen hot ropes that covered both of us.

Emily lay against me, panting heavily. I felt my seed sticking between us like a glue as it dripped down our bellies and thighs. She was breathing like she'd just finished a marathon, and I was right there with her, sucking in air. My prick still felt hard as a rock. It had barely subsided when she eased herself off me and slid her hand free from her panties.

She moved her arms around me; I thought she was going to untie me but she just wrapped them around my waist and nuzzled her head into my throat. "That was so hot, baby," she whispered.

"I know," I told her. But even in the few seconds after my orgasm, some clarity was rushing in and I felt a twinge of doubt. *What the fuck was that?* I wondered. *Was that weird?* But I couldn't deny her words had turned me on like crazy. Everything about her made me crazy. And as she lay against me with a sweet and happy smile, nuzzling my neck and holding me close, I thought anything would be worth it as long as I could have her.

And then she was untying me, and hauling me too my feet. I took advantage of my free hands to wrap her up tight in my arms and squeeze her close. "Now that I'm free, it's payback time," I warned her.

Emily giggled and squeezed my butt. "I can't wait."

VI

We made love two more times that same night. The first, after our leisurely dinner of some salmon and a bottle of wine, was right there on that same couch where she'd teased me. We were watching the freshly fed fire crackle and I slid my hand up her waist and pulled her close to me and then I was between her legs on the couch, working myself into her deep and hard while she squeezed me tight from beneath.

The second was after our twilight soak in the hot tub on the deck, sleepy from the wine and warm water. We entwined in bed as I slowly worked myself inside her. There was no talk during, and no urgency. Just the serene sensation of her stretching open to take me, the rhythmic flow inside her, pushing deeper and wider as our eyes flickered together in the dark. Afterward we dozed off with me still inside her and holding her tight to me. It wasn't until an hour later when she had to pee that she shook herself free of me. I slid out with a trickle of cum- how did I still have *any* left?- and waited for her return so I could snuggle her back to sleep.

We woke up in a loving nest of matted hair and sweat-damp flesh and tangled limbs the next day. I kissed her back to sleep and crept out of bed to make a pot of coffee in the french press we brought. And as the kettle heated on the stove, I looked out over the fog rolling up the Blue Ridge hills, dazzling in the fullness of their fiery fall display.

I brought two steaming mugs back to bed. Emily

gave me a sweet and sleepy smile and wrapped her arms around my waist as I sat back against the headboard. I took the first rich sip of coffee with my fingers tangled in her soft blonde hair. "Morning, baby," she whispered to me.

"Morning," I said, brushing her soft cheek. "It's gorgeous out."

She murmured happily and and nestled her head into my lap. "What's for breakfast?"

"Hash browns and a big omelet,"I told her. "I'll get the cast iron going. Plus," I added as if telling her a secret. "I brought a tube of pumpkin cinnamon rolls."

She gave a happy squeal and sniggled closer to me. "That sounds perfect.".

"Well, we have a big day," I said, passing her my coffee cup. "Need to fuel up if we're going to make it all the way to Shining Rock."

She took a gulp of coffee and set it aside. Then she

pounced into my lap and squeezed me tight in her arms. "Well, guess you better get breakfast started," she said, burrowing into me. "Go on."

I tried to shift my body but she was pinning me too tight. I smiled and let her restrain me- there was no way I was going to pull away from that sweet embrace. She was a messy angel with her eyes squeezed shut and her crazy morning hair and her flushed cheeks. I just held her back, savoring the feeling of her smooth skin in my hands.

As she snuggled deeper into me, one of her hands slid around my front and started creeping up my shorts. "What are you doing down there?" I asked, rubbing her head.

"I know what I really want for breakfast," she said. Her fingers found me, and my cock began unfurling in her hand. "I want this big breakfast sausage."

I couldn't believe she was trying to get me going again. I let her tug down my shorts and release my cock, which was stiffening quickly. "Look at that," she said. "You're so hard already."

"I can't believe I have anything left after last night."

"Yeah, jesus," Emily giggled. "I could feel you dripping out of me all night. I think I still have your cum inside me." She rolled over and stuck her hand between her legs to feel around beneath the covers, a dirty smirk playing on her face.

"Oh, god," she said with an exaggerated grimace. "Yep. It's everywhere."

She was laying on her back with her hand between her legs, and I was still kneeling by her head with my cock out. I stroked it idly while I watched her feel around between her legs. "It's like I'm wet," she said. "Look." She held up two glistening fingers in a v-shape. The sight made me twitch, and I continued stroking my rapidly swelling cock.

She smiled as she watched me rub myself, and twiddled her fingers back and forth. "You like that?"

"Can't you tell?" I asked. My cock told the whole story. I stretched it down at the base, letting it stand straight out from me.

"Your cock looks huge from this angle," Emily giggled. She was almost cross-eyed, looking up at it from her back. Her fingers slipped between her legs again and I could see her rubbing around her naked, swelling vulva. Her eyes slipped shut as she began focusing on the pleasure. I went on stroking as she played with herself, and soon we were both getting ourselves worked up.

She opened her eyes and smirked up at me. Without a word, she opened her mouth up at me. I wasn't going to miss this unmistakeable invitation, and I scooted around and fed my hard cock into her mouth. Her mouth was so soft and warm closing around it, her tongue massaging against my cock head. She continued fingering herself while sucking me softly, slathering my shaft with spit.

Then she abruptly stopped and rolled onto her side. She leaned off the bed and reached for the floor to root around inside her bag. Her peachy butt was pointed toward me, and I could see her puffed up vulva and her ass directed toward me. I couldn't resist landing a smack on that perfect butt. Emily gave a playful yelp, then rolled back on her back.

She was holding a thick silicone vibrator she must have retrieved from her bag. She snapped it on, and it began to hum. Without a word, she took my cock in her hand and fed it back inside her mouth. As she sucked my cock, she began to rub the humming vibrator up and down against her vulva. The flush was rising in her face.

The view of her from above was magnificent. She was laid out on her back, her pretty mouth wrapped around my cock, her hair scattered across the bed like a halo, her slender lithe and perfect small ripe breasts on full display, her tight stomach contorting with every thrust of the vibrator inside her pussy. My cock was throbbing hard as she sucked me down while she started to fuck herself harder with the vibrator.

She took my cock from her mouth and worked it with her hand while looking up at me. "I love getting filled up from both ends," she said, swallowing my cock down again. I could feel it pushing deep toward the back of her throat. "It feels like I have a cock in my pussy and my mouth."

"Have you ever done that before?" I asked, my fingers in her hair. Her mouth was opening up for me as she fucked herself and i started thrusting my hips to work my cock into her mouth.

"Get spitroasted?" she gasped when letting me go again. She smacked my cock against her tongue while grinning up at me. "A couple times. I loved it," she went on, sucking me between thoughts. "It feels so fucking good to get filled up from both sides." She was working the vibrator in a steady deep rhythm now, in and out at an angle that was stretching her wide.

"This one time," she said, then took my cock deep in her throat. "I went to this punk show" *gulp* "and the guys in the band were so hot" *gulp* "so I hung around after the show to talk to them" *gulp* "and I ended up going into the dressing room with the singer and the guitar player."

"What band was it?" I asked stupidly.

Emily just laughed. "You've never heard of them," she told me. She stroked my fully lubed up cock with the vibrator thrust deep inside her, holding it still to let the vibrations run through her body. "I got down on my knees and started sucking both of them," she told me, hungrily kissing up my shaft. "Switching back and forth between their dicks."

A delicious pressure was building inside my cock, Her mouth was so soft and warm against me, teasing me as she kissed me up and down. "Then the guitarist grabbed me under my arms and just picked me up," she said, her lips dragging over my cock as she talked. "He was so fucking jacked. I felt tiny in his arms."

She's thinking about him right now, I realized, watching her drive the vibrator into herself deep and hard while she kissed me. I couldn't be too upset about that because i was so turned on watching her fuck herself and suck my dick. I didn't care.

"He threw me onto this couch in the dressing room," she said. "I was wearing this little skirt and he reached up it and just ripped off my panties. Before I knew it he was shoving his dick inside me." She gasped, pumping the vibrator in deeper. "Fuck, he was so huge. I thought he was going to split me in half."

She took my cock back in her mouth and sucked me up and down. "Just as I was getting used to it, the guitarist came up to me and stuck his dick in my face." *Gulp gulp* "so I started sucking it, of course." She gave me a dirty smile. "He was huge too. They both were."

Bigger than me? I wondered for a second, but the the thought was gone as I lost myself in the pleasure. She groaned with pleasure against the vibrator and kissed her way down to my balls. "It was so intense getting stretched open from both ends like that. And by two guys I'd never even talked to before. I felt like such a dirty slut."

"Yeah, you are," I murmured, running my hands through her hair. "My dirty girl."

"You like it, don't you?" she said, licking up my balls again and rubbing my cock with her hand. "You like hearing about what a dirty slut I've been?" She swallowed my cock down deeper and let me pump it inside her throat while she thrust in with the vibrator.

I gripped her throat with my hand and pinned her to the bed, fucking her mouth. "That's right," I growled, thrusting my hips forward and watching my cock disappear into her mouth. "You dirty slut. You little fucking whore." Her face was completely flushed red as she drove herself crazier with the vibrator.

She pulled her head back and my cock slipped from her mouth, dripping with her saliva. "Oh fuck," she gasped. "I wish this was a real dick in me right now," she moaned, stroking my slippery cock.

"I bet you do, you little slut," I said, gripping her hair. I forced my cock back in her throat and fucked her hard. She was moaning with pleasure, grinding her hips hungrily while I stretched her throat out.

"Fuck yes," she gasped when she came up for air again. "Your dick feels so good in my throat. I wish I could have it in my pussy too." She jerked my cock while she talked. "Those guys fucked me so hard. I couldn't even walk or talk after. They took turns fucking me from both sides. It was so hard and rough. They were completely using me like the dirtiest little whore. And I loved it."

She deepthroated me rapidly a few more times before pulling out to say more. Her voice had a singleminded hungry desperation and I could tell she was getting herself close. "I loved getting bent over and fucked in that skirt while my mouth got filled. They were pulling my hair and spanking me and treating me like such a slut. And I couldn't get enough of their big beautiful cocks."

"You're such a slut," I told her. "Such a cock hungry little whore."

"Yes, I am," she moaned. "I was so horny I never wanted them to stop. But I wanted their cum so bad." She gave a shuddering breath and I knew she was close.

"Where did they cum?"

"In my pussy," she moaned, "and all over my face." She swallowed down my cock again. "The guitarist shot a huge load inside me. And then the singer made me get back down on my knees. I could feel the cum dripping out of my cunt while he fucked my face. And then he pulled out and covered my face with the biggest load ever."

Her rapid breathing increased, and her body was starting to tingle. "It felt so good getting covered in his load. And then I had to go out of the dressing room and I knew it was still in my hair and on my face. I felt like the dirtiest whore in the world."

"Fuck yeah," I groaned, working my shaft near her face.

"This really turns you on to hear about?" she moaned.

"So much," I told her.

"You're such a pervert,:" she said. "Dirty boy getting off on hearing about your girlfriend getting double teamed by two strangers." She wiggled her hips. "I'm so fucking close," she groaned. "I want your cock inside me."

I didn't need a second invitation. I slid around between her legs and pulled the vibrator out of her. My cock was so stiff I could see every vein on it. "Hurry up,"

"Yeah? You need this inside you?" I rubbed my cock up her pussy, just barely stretching the entrance.

"Come on," she begged. "Please, fuck me. I'm so close."

She moaned when my fully hard cock slid all the way inside her in a long, smooth motion. She was so wet and open for me I didn't even need to take my time. But I took the vibrator and held it to her lips. "Suck it."

She took the vibrator in her mouth and sucked it while I started fucking her, hard and deep. I thrust the vibrator into the back of her throat, savoring her dirty groans as I started driving my cock hard against her. "Oh fuck," she cried, bucking her hips against me. "I'm so close."

I cut her words off by shoving the vibrator deep in

her mouth. She just made little muffled moans as I felt her entire body tense against my cock as it daggered her. She was trying to cry out around the silicone in her throat but couldn't. Her cunt was so hot and warm against me as I fucked her hard and the pressure was irresistible. "Oh, fuck," I groaned. "I'm going to-"

"Not yet," she cried, but it was too late. My hardness broke; my cock exploded deep inside her. She wrapped her arms around me and held me close as I came inside her, flooding her.

"Oh my god," I groaned, collapsing against her. "Jesus."

She pulled the vibrator from her throat and giggled. "Wow," she said. "You must have really liked that."

I nuzzled up against her cheek and kissed her face up and down. "That was incredible." I pulled away from her, my cock slipping out from her soaked pussy. A trail of cum gushed out of her and dripped down her ass. *I fucked that up.*

She read my sheepish expression right away. "What?" she asked.

"Oh, nothing, I said, still panting. "I'm sorry."

"For what?"

"Well, I mean…" I stammered. "Did you… I mean, you didn't-"

Emily waved her hand. "It's ok," she laughed. "I don't have to cum every time."

"Yeah, but you were so close," I said.

"Yeah I was," she laughed. Her fingers ran to her pussy again and she idly toyed with it. "I still am."

"You want me to-"

Emily pursed her lips. That mischievous playful smirk played on her face. "Well," she said. "I mean, I did tell you not to cum and you did it anyway. Bad boy."

"I'm sorry," I said, getting into the spirit.

"Well, you better not leave me with blue balls." She spread her pussy open, the trail of fresh cum splattering on her thighs. "Better get down there and finish the job."

I burrowed my face between her legs right away and slipped my tongue against her. I could taste my own cum, salty and pungent, mixed in with the ripe aroma of her unwashed cunt. My fingers slipped inside her as I began to lick her greedily. She was already on the edge.

"That's right," she said, grinding her hips in my face. "Eat that cunt. With all your own cum in it. You dirty pervert." She bucked her hips so hard it was like she was fucking my mouth. "You dirty boy. Getting so horny listening to my slutty stories. I bet you wish that was someone else's cum you were licking out of my pussy right now."

I couldn't protest, my mouth was too full of her full heavenly cunt. She gripped me by the hair and ground her face against me. "Dirty boy. You better earn in, you nasty little pervert." I crooked my fingers inside her, stretching her cunt while licking her clit.

She moaned and leaned back against the pillow. "That's a good boy," she said. "Good little cum-sucker. Don't stop, you're getting me close."

And before long a wave of pressure swelled then broke over her body in a gasping shudder. Her cunt twitched and pulsed like a wild thing against my fingers as the orgasm washed over her body. I burrowed deeper, trying to ignore the feeling and taste of my cum as I drove her through the orgasm.

Finally, the pleasure subsided and she lay back panting with a happy smile. "Good boy," she breathed, vigorously scratching my hair. She giggled and stretched against the bed. "Ok," she said. "It's time for a real breakfast."

VII

We lingered over our breakfast in sleepy happy

quiet. The cabin had such large windows that it seemed like we were enclosed in a glass dome surrounded by the stunning Appalachian landscape in its full autumn splendor. The fiery reds and oranges were spread across the rolling hills as far as we could see, and the midmorning sun revealed a sky as light and blue as a dream.

I spread my maps out over the table and we discussed the plan for the day. Since we'd whiled away our morning, we knew we'd have to get moving if we wanted to make our hiking circuit before dark. But the cabin was so cozy warm and our desire for each other so strong that we were both tempted to forget the whole hiking adventure and spend the entire day in bed. But the day was too pretty to waste indoors.

I pulled on some hiking gear and started gathering our needs for a daypack while Emily got ready in the bedroom. *Granola bars, water, extra layers...* I was focusing so much on not forgetting anything I hardly noticed when Emily emerged from the bedroom. But when I finally looked up, she blew me away. She wore a pair of black leggings that clung to her shapely legs and hips, with a thermal shirt that also hugged her every curve. Her hair was swept up under the same beanie she was wearing the night before, with blonde wisps kissing along her pearl cheeks and neck. She looked so sleek and strong and outdoorsy and wild and beautiful, everything I could ever have imagined from a girl but never dreamed I could actually have in my life. I can still picture how she looked in that moment, cheeks flushed, eyes shining, smiling at me, ready for our adventure together.

I drove us down the winding mountain backroads with her small soft hand in mind, weaving through the gorgeous autumn scenery. We rode along the spine of Appalachians on the Blue Ridge Parkway, taking in sweeping views of the lit-up valleys of the Pisgah National Forest. Every mountain curve exposed a new valley of lush fire and the faraway peaks on the other side. At times it seemed like we were coasting on the clouds, looking down on the earth from so far above.

We shared a comfortable quiet on the drive, pointing out the beautiful features of the rolling hills but otherwise speaking very little. Jason Isbell played softly through the speakers; sunlight danced off the windshield. I stole glances at her constantly, only to find her eyes were on me as well. Whenever our gazes met like this we smiled and looked away, embarrassed by the strength of our infatuation.

Her dirty stories from before were still on my mind, and I wasn't sure how to feel about them. There was something so wrong about knowing those things about her past. And something very wrong about how much they turned me on. But Emily was so gorgeous and so sweet. I was caught up in my desire for her and the undeniably arousing image of her in the throes of passion. Even the part of me that reacted with jealous frustration at the thought of someone else enjoying her seemed to somehow just feed into my attraction to her and my need to have her. It was all confusing, but I knew that I could accept anything as long as I got to have her.

The parking lot was full already, thanks to our late start. I squeezed us into a spot along the roadside and we hopped out of the car. The balsam smell blended with the crisp air of fall and we sucked in deep, invigorating breaths. We stretched our legs out, limbering up for the hike. Emily bent down into a deep squat and then let out a little giggle.

"What's up?" I asked.

She rolled her eyes. "I just felt a gush. You're gonna be dripping out of me this entire hike."

I helped her up from her squat and planted a kiss on her lips. "I love that," I whispered in her ear.

"I bet you do," she said. "Dirty boy. Ready?"

And so we headed down the Art Loeb train into the Shining Rock Wilderness. The air was crisp and cool, but the bright sunshine promised to keep us warm. The only sound for the first stretch of our hike was the crunch of our boots on the packed dirt trail. I walked a little distance ahead of Emily, guiding us along the trail until the forest opened up. As we gained elevation the trees cleared and the hillside was just a grassy bald, revealing incredible expansive views of the surrounding mountains of the Pisgah.

Finally, we reached the crest of Tennant Mountain.

From there, the vast scenery of the rolling mountains surrounded us on all sides. It felt like we could see forever in each direction. Emily snuggled up beside me to warm herself up from the cool wind that blew hard high up on the mountains, and I pulled her in close to me to warm her up.

She looked up at me with her sweet shining eyes and I felt the full force of love coming at me in a way that melted my heart. "This is amazing," she told me.

I pulled her close and kissed her on the forehead. "I'm glad you're with me."

"Me too."

We carried on the hike for several more miles, taking in another panoramic view at the top of the Black Balsam Knob. We pressed onward into the wilderness, chatting intermittently but mostly keeping quiet. The beauty of the views and the difficult trekking kept us occupied.

After several hours and miles of hiking, we came

around a bend. Across the valley was an enormous rock mound the size of a stadium, crowned with a forest of fiery orange and red trees. The whole cliffside seemed to glitter from the quartz embedded all across its massive prominence. Emily seized my hand and pointed to across the valley to the mountain. "There it is!" she said. "Shining Rock!"

"Wow," I told her. "It's incredible."

"There's a Cherokee legend about Shining Rock," Emily said. "Before the trail of tears. A band of Cherokees families fled from soldiers into the Pisgah. The soldiers chased them all the way into the forest. Probably over some of those trails we just covered. They were drawing close, and the Cherokee were running out of places to go. They had their children with them, and the elderly, and they couldn't run anymore. But all they needed to do was make it to Shining Rock."

"Did they hide on top of it?"

"No," Emily said. "They walked right into it. The Shining Rock opened up and let them pass through into another world, where they'd be safe." Her voice was so solemn that it seemed she almost believed this story herself.

"Do you think that's true?"

Emily gave a mysterious shrug. Then a big smile crossed her face. "I'm starving," she said. "Let's eat here."

I laid out the blanket and started arranging our tortillas and peanut butter and snacks. Emily took off her hiking shoes and wiggled her toes luxuriously. "Oh man," she said. "These doggies are *ripe.*"

We ate lunch there in the view of the Shining Rock and the mountains of the Pisgah. And then Emily turned to me and asked, "do you feel weird about any of that stuff we talked about?"

I knew what she was talking about, but for some reason I played it coy. "I don't believe the Cherokee really disappeared"

She pursed her lips. "You know," she said. "The

stories I was telling you."

I thought for a minute. I genuinely did not know the real answer. How *did* it make me feel? Confused, I guess. "I don't know," I told her. "It's strange. In the moment I think it's so hot and exciting. But I guess it's kind of weird to feel that way, isn't it?"

Emily looked down. "I guess." She didn't seem to like that answer very much.

I thought some more. "I guess I'm a little embarrassed," I said. "It feels so wrong to be turned on by those stories. But *everything* about you turns me on. And I guess I should be threatened by your past experiences, and part of me kind of is, but-"

"Why threatened?" Emily interrupted.

"Just worried I won't be good enough," I told her.

Emily rolled her eyes, but her smile was sweet. "I already told you," she said. "There's a lot more to a relationship than sex. You're a really sweet guy. There's nothing to worry about."

"Every guy wants to be the best," I went on. "We all want to be the biggest stud ever."

"That's so silly," Emily said. "It's not a competition. Plus, you've fucked other girls too."

My stories were nothing compared to hers, but I didn't mention that. I just told her "You're right, and I know it's silly. It doesn't really even bother me that much. I mean, listening to your stories turned me on like crazy. It's just that it feels like I'm *supposed* to be bothered by it."

Emily thought about this for a minute. "Can I tell you something?"

"Sure."

"I've worried a lot about how I'm *supposed* to feel about sex. Ever since I was a kid, my parents made me feel so guilty about it. And I wasn't even having sex! Ever since then, I've felt so conflicted about it. Like I wanted it so bad, but I also felt so ashamed of it. Even after I started acting on it, I still felt bad about myself. I thought it would make me feel in control, but I could never shake that shame about it."

"But you seem so open about it," I said.

"That's what I'm trying to say," she told me. "I guess I always worried that my past would stop me from having a real relationship. I thought I was damaged goods because… well, because any guy I wanted to date would be turned off by my history."

"But opening up to you about it has felt so good. Even if it's just in dirty talk. I feel like it helps me get over a lot of that stuff. It feels so good to own it, and to tell you about it, and to have you respond so well to it. Like, knowing that it turns you on is such a huge relief to me."

"I'm crazy about you," I told her. "I don't care about your past."

"I hope not," she said. "I feel like it's kind of unfair. Telling you about it in the heat of the moment like that. I hope you'd be able to tell me about it if it bothered you."

"Oh, definitely," I told her. "I would say something."

"Good," she said. "Because, well… I love telling you about that stuff. It makes me feel so much better about everything. Not having to hide my past."

"I feel a little weird about how much it turns me on," I admitted. "But that's just because it *does* turn me on. Like crazy. Imagining you in all those different situations… getting fucked in all those different ways… and seeing how turned on it makes you to talk about it… I just picture you in those situations and it drives me wild."

"It really does?"

"So much. Just like all the teasing and the denial and all that stuff… something about all of that just makes me crazy. I love it."

Emily suddenly leaned against me, burying her

shoulder into my chest. She snuggled me tight up against me, nuzzling her face into my neck. "I'm just happy I found you," she whispered to me. "Thanks for being so understanding."

I squeezed her hands and pulled her closer to me. "It's easy," I told her. "With you, I feel like I could be down for just about anything."

"Anything?" Her tone sent a shiver down my spine, wondering what possible things she could be thinking about. But I really didn't care what it was.

"As long as I have you," I answered.

She leaned in to kiss me on the neck. Her hot breath in my ear turned into a bite on my earlobe that almost made me yelp with shock. "Well then," she whispered. "I think I have a couple ideas."

"Yeah? Like what?"

Emily cocked her head toward Shining Rock. "Look up there," she said. "I think there's some people."

"The Cherokee?"

"I don't think the Cherokee had binoculars," Emily laughed.

I squinted across the valley at massive rock formation, its quartz formations glittering in the early afternoon sunlight. "How can you tell they have binoculars?"

"It's one of the most popular birdwatching spots around here," she explained. "I'm sure they've got em." She raised a hand and waved toward the tiny figures on the rock. A minute later, a faint response echoed through the valley. "See?"

Emily's hand was creeping down my leg again. It nestled between my thighs and started rubbing my package through my hiking pants.

"What do you think you're doing?" I asked, but my cock was already responding.

Emily giggled and rubbed harder, feeling my shaft thicken. "Let's give those bird-nerds a show," she whispered huskily in my ear.

"You really want to jerk me off in front of the Audobon Society?"

"No," she said. Then she scooted back on the blanket, hooked her thumbs in her leggings, and slid them down around her thighs. "I want you to eat my pussy in front of them."

I could hear the voices shouting across the valley, deep male hollering. I knew they could see Emily's naked thighs and ass through the binoculars. The thought of being watched while going down on her made the hair stand up on my neck. But I couldn't actually *see* the guys who were watching. Besides- I looked over at Emily. She was laying back, propped on her elbows, eyebrows cocked suggestively at me. She slid a hand between her naked thighs and spread her pussy open for me. It was too much to resist.

I laid between her legs and gripped her smooth

thighs in my hands. Her cunt had a dizzying aroma from our hike. I inhaled deeply. The rich scent was so intoxicating it felt like it was flowing straight into my cock and inflating it like a balloon. I savored her smell for a while, delicately running my nose up and down her slit. The voices from the Shining Rock across the valley hooted in appreciation.

"Come on," Emily said, gripping my hair tight in her fist. "Stop teasing." She forced my face up to her cunt. I obediently ran my tongue up her open pussy, and she shivered in response. Soon my tongue was burrowing deep into her. I licked her up and down. She was slick as a silk between her lips.

I stretched her taut and teased her clit while massaging my fingers on her entrance. "Fuck yeah," she moaned. I slipped my fingers into her, feeling her stretch out for me. She arched her back on the picnic blanket, driving her hips into my face. The shouting voices carried over the rolling hills, encouraging me to go deeper.

Finally she pushed my head away from her. "Get up," she ordered. I sat up on my knees at once. I was still wiping her juices from my lips when she reached down and unbuckled my pants. She tugged my zipper down. *I'm about to get a blowjob,* I thought, and my dick twitched happily.

But instead, Emily seized me by the shoulders and threw me roughly to the ground. I was so shocked, I hadn't even spoken when she reached down and jerked down my pants. Despite my fear and the cool mountain air, my cock was standing at full attention. I looked up at Emily, and found only a crazy hunger in her eyes.

She mounted me, slipped her hand between her legs to find my cock, and positioned it right at the dripping center of her cunt. Her slide down my pole was such sweet incredible warmth. Her pussy felt like a warm massage, so tight yet so soft and gentle. I could feel every inch of her opening up for me as she slowly worked down my shaft. The hoots from across the valley increased. I was sure they must have an incredible view of her ripe full ass as it slid down my cock.

She nestled up against me for a second, the full length of my shaft sunk deep inside her. But then she was sliding up again. We both gasped at the sensation of our bodies clinging together. She paused at the top, the tip of my cock just barely clinging to her. Then she slid back down again, thrusting me deep inside her.

Soon she was working herself up into a rhythm. She bucked her hips against me, forcing my cock to stretch her open at the entrance. She pinned my arms to the ground and rode hard. The smack of her butt against my thighs echoed in the crisp mountain air, blending with the shouts from across the valley. I couldn't move beneath her. Her grip was too tight. I just laid back and felt her work me inside her over and over, the glorious sliding up and down rhythm of her pounding hips driving me wild.

I could sense my orgasm was building inside me as she worked herself into me. Her panting moans grew more frantic as she drove herself into ecstasy, and her cunt was sopping wet, sucking my cock deep inside it. That hungry yearning need I felt from her, that I saw in her eyes as she rode me, drove me completely crazy, but I could not free my hands from her grip. She pounded away, taking my cock deep inside her over and over. The pressure in me was becoming unbearable. I was reaching my limits and losing control. "Oh, god,' I groaned. "I'm getting-"

Emily stopped abruptly. Her head whipped around to the side, and she peered off into the woods with wide eyes. She saw something. Suddenly she was scrambling off me. "Pull your pants up!" she hissed. I could hear footsteps nearby. Someone was there. Oh fuck.

I pulled my pants up past my throbbing cock and did my best to button them. Meanwhile Emily was struggling her leggings back up her thighs. The footsteps were drawing closer, crunch-crunching over the path toward us. Emily managed to slip the leggings up over her peach butt just before the footsteps emerged from the trees.

A deep man's voice spoke up. "How are you folks doing on this beautiful day?" Even though we knew someone was coming, the voice still startled us.

In front of us stood a U.S. Forest Service ranger in that olive-green mountie hat. He was an older guy, maybe in his fifties, with a stout belly and a smirk beneath his moustache that told us he probably knew exactly what we'd been doing.

"Oh, it's amazing," Emily said. Her face was flushed bright red and her voice was breathless. "We were just having a picnic here."

The ranger assumed a wide stance and hitched his thumbs in his belt. He examined the scene deliberately, his eyes running over the disheveled blanket and our flushed and sweaty faces. I thought I could feel his eyes on the bulge in my pants that somehow wouldn't go away. It felt like the eiffel tower sticking out. I tried to stick my hands in my pockets and stretch out the fabric to hide it, but it didn't help.

The ranger's eyes ran slowly up Emily's body, lingering on all her curves. "Well, it sure looks like you kids are having fun out here," he said. He cleared his throat with authority. "Now, I got a complaint over my radio here. Said there were a couple young people stemming the rose out here, in a manner of speaking." He raised his eyebrows. "You wouldn't happen to know anything about that, would you?"

"Oh, of course not!" said Emily breathlessly.

The ranger looked at me. His eyes were expectant. "Uh, no sir," I stammered. My heart was pounding in my chest. "I haven't heard anything."

The ranger squinted at me. I could feel his eyes boring into me, melting straight through my lie like a laser. He scanned over to Emily with the same scrutinizing gesture. Then his eyes ran back to the ground. We followed them and found they were focused on something laying in the grass. My eyes went wide when I recognized the little pink bundle of cotton. *Emily's panties.*

"Those yours, miss?" the ranger asked.

"Nope," said Emily, her face innocent.

His eyes flickered over to me. "Maybe they're yours, boy."

I gulped. "No sir."

The ranger flashed a wolfish smile. "Well then.

Guess it's just some litter."

"We'll get rid of them," I offered. "I've got a trash bag."

"Better do that," he said. He started reaching for a notebook in his waistband. "And then I'm going to have to ask both of you a few questions. Alone."

Suddenly Emily broke in. "Unless you want to take them for us, Mr. Ranger."

I looked over at her in shock. Her face glowed with the innocent mischief smile that I could never resist. I was sure the ranger couldn't, either.

Sure enough, the ranger looked like he was about to fall over from shock. Then a wide grin broke over his face. "Don't mind if I do," he said. He started to stoop down to grab the panties, but Emily was too quick. She shot out her bare foot and stepped on top of them, blocking his reach.

"Hold on," she said. "I'll let you have them, but

under one condition."

The ranger grumbled back upright. "Yeah?" he said. "What is it?"

"We've got to get back to our car," she said. "So we're not going to have time to stick around and answer a bunch of questions. You can have them if you let us leave right now."

The ranger pursed his lips at her, considering the offer. No doubt he had been taking pleasure at the thought of getting her alone and interviewing her. He looked back down at the panties pinned underneath her foot and thought. "Fine," he said, holding out his hand. "Give them here."

With the precision of a dancer, Emily gripped the panties between her toes. Then she flicked out her foot, flinging the panties. They landed perfectly in his outstretched hand. He unfurled them with both hands, admiring the pink lacy pattern. "I can't believe you were hiking in these," he said. "They must have got real dirty."

"Filthy," Emily answered in a seductive growl. Then she shot the ranger a pointed look. "Well, we've got some cleaning up to do here," she said, gesturing at the remnants of our picnic on the blanket. "But thanks for keeping the forest safe, Mr. Ranger."

"You're welcome," the Ranger murmured. He shot me a contemptuous smirk, then held the panties up to his nose. He didn't break eye contact with me as he inhaled deeply. My stomach churned with frustration, but my cock was still so thick and full from my arousal earlier. I said nothing, and instead busied myself cleaning up the picnic scene.

"Be good, kids," the ranger told us. "And watch out. There's perverts out here in the woods."

VIII

I was worried about how Emily would react once the ranger left. But as soon as he disappeared into the woods, she pounced on me. Kisses smothered my face

119

from my cheek to my neck. "That was so crazy!" she said.

"Yeah," I agreed, a little uneasy. "How did you feel about that?"

Emily squeezed me around the neck. "Well it got us out of trouble," she said. "I can't believe we almost got caught having sex!"

"I can't believe we were being watched."

"I think we gave them a pretty good show," said Emily. She planted a kiss on my lips, then released me. "Do you think that ranger's gonna jerk off with my panties?"

There was a twinge in my stomach like a pit just opened up. I pictured that ranger's smirk as he held the panties to his nose, and I knew he would definitely be enjoying them later. I felt a surge of anger and frustration at the thought. "What a pervert."

Emily giggled. "Says the guy who was just eating my pussy in front of the whole Audobon Society," she teased.

I couldn't believe how giddy Emily seemed. The
entire experience seemed to have charged her with a
manic energy, and she talked unceasingly as we started
hiking back down the trail. I was more subdued.
Something about the experience gnawed at me, but I
couldn't place exactly what it was.

"He thought those panties were yours!" Emily
laughed, poking me hard on the side.

"Not my style," I said, trying to laugh it off.

"Oh, bullshit," said Emily. She landed a hard slap
on my butt. "I bet this peach would look real cute in a pair
of lacy panties." I tried to not respond, but she pressed me.
"Did you ever try on a pair of girl's underwear before?"

Sweat beaded on my brow. Emily was talking so
fast I couldn't keep up. I was still in shock from the
encounter with the park ranger and the show we'd put on
for the bird watchers on Shining Rock. And now
everything she was saying made me nervous. But her

giddy attitude was infectious, and despite my misgivings I couldn't help but play along with her. "Not yet," I answered.

This cracked Emily up. She gave my butt another slap with a firm squeeze. "Oh, I can't wait to see that," she said. "I wonder what else of mine you'd look cute in."

I swallowed. "Dang, that really got you excited, huh?"

"I know it got you excited, too," Emily said. Suddenly her hand darted around me and squeezed my cock. I gave a startled yelp that made her giggle even harder. "Look at that big cock!" she said. "Was it frustrating, getting so close while you were fucking me? I bet you're still on the edge."

I had to admit I was. Even knowing that all the eyes of the birdwatchers were on us hadn't stopped me from getting worked up almost to bursting when she was riding me. And the forest ranger interruption only increased the frustration she was reawakening in me.

Emily teased me the entire way back down the Ivestor Gap trail. Hours of lurid stories and dirty comments, all punctuated by ass slaps and crotch gropes that made me feel like I was being herded down the trail. She sensed my embarrassment at the predicament she was putting me in, and pressed her advantage as far as she could take it. But there was a sweetness in her teasing. A shining in her eyes that let me know she was just having fun pressing my buttons.

It was too easy for her. Every so often I'd be worked up to the point where I seized her and started kissing her lips. She'd play along for a minute, her hands running all over my body. And then she's pull away abruptly and scold me for being a dirty boy. It was dizzying, the constant push-pull of teasing. She had me wrapped completely around her finger.

And as the afternoon sun's slanted rays hurried us along, she told me more stories about her past. Stories about pictures she'd posted of herself. One night stands. Threesomes. Having sex with girls. Posting videos of herself getting fucked.

"You were a porn star?"

"Amateur," she said, with no small hint of pride. "And I never showed my face. So who knows," she winked. "Maybe you've jerked off to me before."

Emily's litany of lewdness kept me frothing at the mouth the rest of the hike back. I couldn't believe the effect her words had on me. I should have been disgusted, horrified, jealous, angry. But instead I just felt the relentless frustration of wanting her so bad. It was all I could think about. Each new revelation of depravity only intensified my hunger for her.

I was practically delirious by the time we reached my car. The day had slipped to evening, and the bright autumn leaves glowed with the rich evening redness all across the valleys of the Pisgah. There was a faint campfire smell in the chilly air. We were both worn out from the many miles we'd clocked, and we both groaned as we settled into the car.

Emily cranked the heat as I started weaving us back onto the Blue Ridge Parkway and home to the cabin.

Before long, the car was toasty warm. Emily slipped off her boots and socks, then put her bare feet in my lap. Once again my cock sprang to full attention. Emily pressed a dainty bare foot into my stiff prick through my hiking pants. Once she felt it, she started teasing me again. Whispering dirty stories as she massaged my cock with her feet, delighting in tormenting me.

The drive back to our cabin was somehow even more gorgeous than the trip to the mountains. The evening light cast a magical glow that lit up the rocks and trees of the valleys. The entire world was on fire. And I was, too. Burning for Emily, who stoked the flames of my passion easily with her constant stream of dirty thoughts.

The minute we stepped foot in the cabin again I tried to take her. I pushed her up against the door and kissed her flush on the mouth. She let me make out with her for a while, arching her back and leaning into my hands that ran up her thighs and stomach. But she resisted when I tried to pull her leggings down. "Dirty boy," she scolded, pushing me away. "We'll never make it to dinner if you can't keep your hands to yourself."

"I want you so fucking bad," I told her, nuzzling close to her neck with my stiff prick pressing up against her thigh.

She just laughed and pushed me back. "That's good," she told me. "Keep wanting me. You can have me after dinner." She scrutinized my dirty hiking outfit. "Aren't you going to get cleaned up?"

I sighed and pulled away from her. "You kill me." I headed to the bathroom, stripping off my clothes along the way and dropping them on the cabin floor.

Just before I closed the bathroom door behind me, Emily thrust her hand out to block me. "Hold on," she commanded.

"What?"

Emily flashed that mischievous smile. "No jerking off in there."

It was like she read my mind. I lathered myself down in the hot shower, trying not to over-excite my heavy prick. My hunger for Emily was sharper than the real hunger I felt gnawing in my stomach. I was so tempted to get out of the shower and go find her. Throw her on the bed and ravage her. As I showered my mind drifted back to all the dirty stories she told me on our hike. Had she really done all that? Been gangbanged by a college hockey team? Eaten a girl out on a subway car? Seduced a professor at her school? I couldn't stop picturing her doing all those things, nor could I shake the memory of her breathless voice telling me all of it. Instinctively my hand ran down to my soapy cock and stroked it. It was heavy from arousal.

Just as I was starting to work myself fully hard, there was a sharp rapping on the door. "Are you being good in there?" Emily asked though the door.

A rush of panic ran through me like an electric jolt. "No!" I insisted. Then I quickly finished rinsing off the soap and turned off the shower. I felt like a little boy who'd been caught doing something naughty. It was so strange.

As I was drying myself with a fluffy towel, the

doorknob turned. Emily stood on the threshold, fully naked. The sight sent a feverish pulse racing through my body. Everything about her was taut and lean and windswept from our day's adventure. Instinctively. I wrapped the towel around myself to hide my arousal.

Emily smirked. She was fully aware of the effect her nude body had on me. She walked deliberately into the bathroom, directly toward me. The wild scent of her unwashed body sent a tingle down my spine. She tilted her head toward me. A hand shot down to the towel wrapped around me and felt for my thick cock. "I knew it!" she cried triumphantly. "You were jerking off in here."

"No I wasn't," I said, surprised at the insistence in my own voice.

Her fingers squeezed me stiffening prick. "Liar," she teased. "I know what you were up to. Probably jerking off thinking about what we talked about earlier, weren't you?"

I tried to protest, but she squeezed my cock again. "Bad boy," she said. Her eyes were wild, and the sweat-scent on her body intoxicated me. She gripped my face in her other hand, squeezing my cheeks close together. "I'm going to have to lock this thing up if you can't behave," she growled. "What do you think about that?"

Her tight grip on my cheeks prevented me from responding. She squeezed my cock again, harder. Her smile turned to innocent mockery. "Poor boy," she said. "So frustrated and horny. I bet you wish I'd just jerk you off right now. I bet you'd do anything for it."

"Yes," I slurred through the pinch of my cheeks. "Anything."

Her eyes glowed like embers. "Poor, sweet boy," she sang, tightening her grip on my shaft. "Wrapped around my little finger. What am I going to do with you?"

"Please," I begged her. "Please, let me cum."

She cackled and pinched my cheeks together tighter. "You dirty boy," she scolded. "Now I've got to take a shower. Can I trust you to be a good boy and keep your hands off *this*-" she squeezed my cock painfully for emphasis.

"Yes," I gasped. "Yes, I won't touch it."

Emily narrowed her eyes at me. "I don't trust you," she said. She whipped off the corner of my towel, leaving me standing completely naked in the bathroom. Then she seized my cock and tugged it. She pulled me by my dick like a dog on a leash, dragging me toward the door. "Get down on your knees," she ordered.

I obeyed at once. The cool tile floor sent a jolt through my knees. Emily loomed over me like a giantess, looking down with a cruel smile. She was wild and powerful and painfully sexy, staring down at me in all her naked glory. "Lift up your arms."

I raised my hands in the air like I was surrendering. She grabbed my discarded shirt from the floor and twisted it around the doorknob, then dexterously wound it around my wrists. When she finished, I was bound to the doorknob with my hands above my head, totally unable to move. I was completely helpless and desperately aroused by my captivity.

"There we go," said Emily, admiring her handiwork. She watched my struggle against the bonds with glee. "That will keep you from touching yourself while I shower. And I need it so bad."

She stepped toward me, bringing her hips close to my face. I caught the ripe scent of her unwashed cunt as she stood in front of me, her tight slit parted slightly just in front of my face. "Can you smell it?" she asked.

"It smells so good," I said, straining to get my head closer to her.

Emily giggled. "You're such a pervert," she scolded. "Getting off on the smell of my dirty pussy." She prodded my cock with a dainty foot, sending a jolt through my body. "I bet that ranger is doing the same thing right now. Huffing those dirty panties like he needs them to breathe."

She prodded my cock with her foot again, gripping it slightly with her toes. "Yep, he's probably jerking off with them right now," she said, curling her toes around my shaft. "He's probably got em wrapped around his piggy cock and he's working himself up. Just like you wish you could do right now."

I gave a muffled groan as she continued working my cock with her foot. "Silly ranger," she said. "He didn't even try to bargain with me. He just took the first offer." She fixed me with her smouldering eyes. "I would have sucked his cock."

"What?" I gasped. "You-"

"Oh yeah," Emily growled. She released my cock from her toes and stood before me, legs parted. "I would have gotten down on my knees. Just like you are right now."

She took a step closer to me, and the heavenly scent of her cunt had me salivating. She reached down and pinched her vulva between her fingers, standing legs astride like she was holding a cock for a piss. "I would have unbuckled his pants-" she pushed her hips toward me- "taken out his cock-" her pussy was inches from my mouth- "and sucked it right in front of you."

She cast an imperious look down at me. "Don't just stare at it- eat it." She pushed her cunt into my face, pinning me against the door. I obediently ran my tongue into it, tasting the ripe scent she'd built up throughout the day. My hands struggled helplessly in their bonds, and my cock was just as helpless as it strained against my lap.

Emily seized my hair and forced her cunt into my mouth. "Wouldn't you have liked to watch me suck his cock?" she panted, grinding her hips into me. "How would you have felt, watching your slutty girlfriend get down on her knees for another man?"

I couldn't answer- my mouth was fully occupied- but her dizzying taste and my hours of denial had my cock pulsating hard despite my misgivings. "You would have watched it all like a good boy," she went on, jerking my head back so my tongue slid deep inside her. "Ugh, I wish I'd done it," she gasped. "I would have let him fuck my face right in front of you. I would have choked on his big cock until you saw the tears running down my cheeks."

I tried to pull back for air, but she jerked my hair

forward and forced me against her. "Keep sucking, you little whore," she hissed. I worked my aching tongue back inside her while she rubbed the outside of her labia with two spread fingers. "That's right. Let me fuck your face like I wish he'd fucked mine. You greedy little slut."

She was almost in a trance as she ranted at me, working her hips against me in a manic rhythm. The back of my head banged off the bathroom door over and over as she rode my face. My bloodless arms ached above my head. I struggled for breath, reduced to a slobbering mess as she fucked my mouth and degraded me. And despite all the pain, my cock still pulsed with hot hunger, desperate for release.

"Keep it up," she said. "You better make me cum if you ever want me to touch your cock again." I felt the tension build in her and redoubled my efforts, lapping hungrily at her sopping cunt. "Good boy," she groaned. "Oh, my good sweet slutty boy. Getting so turned on listening to me tell you about sucking another man's cock. I wish I'd had you tied up and helpless like this out there in the woods. I would have made you watch while I gobbled down his dick. Can't you picture him shooting a big load all over my cute face?"

She was definitely getting closer. Her voice was ragged and wild, and the wetness of her cunt had intensified until she was dripping down my chin. "Maybe I would have made you lick all his cum off my face. Would you do that, if it meant I finally got to let you cum?"

My cock spasmed desperately against me. "Yes," I grunted through the mouthful of cunt.

Emily laughed breathlessly as she worked herself closer to the edge. "You dirty little pervert. Licking another man's cum from my slutty lips. Maybe I'd even make you help me suck him off. Maybe I'd hold you still and force his cock down your throat. Maybe-" a pressure started to build in her- "maybe- oh fuck, I'm about to cum. Don't you dare fucking stop"

The powerful wave loomed up inside her. I lapped feverishly at her cunt, feeling the tension spread out over her entire body from her clit. And then the wave broke in a shuddering wail that rocked her entire body. I continued licking as spasms of pleasure jolted through her body one after another. The rich taste of her pussy reached new depths of flavor, and my cock twitched helplessly at the sultry cries of pleasure she made as she ground herself through the cascading pleasure.

When she'd had enough, she gently pulled away from my face. I could feel her wetness soaking my lips cheeks and chin, running down my throat in rivulets. She smiled sweetly down at me, her pale cheeks flushed red. "Oh, that felt so good," she giggled. Her fingers were in my hair, ruffling me gently like a puppy. "Good boy."

I was struggling too hard for breath to respond; I just panted up at her, eyes wet, tongue hanging out of my mouth. Her words had reached new depths of depravity, filling my thoughts with a hot shame I could barely process. Yet still my cock was thick and full with desire. She looked down at it and gave a pitying smile. "Poor baby," she soothed. "You must want to cum so bad."

"Please," I begged. I thrashed against the knots binding my wrists over my head, but the struggle was futile. I was reduced completely to a gibbering mess, dying for her to grant me release. And she reveled in it.

"I'm sorry, sweet boy," she said, gently rubbing my head. "But I'm not done with you yet. I'm having too much fun." She stepped away from me, turning to walk toward the shower. The sight of her perfect peach ass working up and down with every step brought tears to my eyes. She bent down deliberately to turn on the shower, flashing me a full view of her still-soaking pussy and tight pink anus. This was only the start of my torture.

I stayed tied to the bathroom door as she showered. She left the curtain open, and I was forced to watch her clean up her perfect body. She never even glanced at me as she took her time washing herself. And she was so deliberately cruel in her wanton display of all her assets. She soaped her breasts lovingly. She massaged body wash into her thighs. She pointed the showerhead into her crotch, moaning as the jets of water cleaned her cunt. She lathered herself with gel and shaved the prickly patches beneath her arms and dotting her thighs, the razor gliding smoothly over her creamy skin. And all the while I struggled in my bondage, cock twitching. Lust for her was eating me alive, breaking me down into mindless frustrated need.

When she finished showering, she took her time drying herself with a fluffy towel. She continued ignoring me as I watched from the floor, not even sparing a single glance as she prepared herself for the evening out. She blew her hair dry. She moisturized her skin, and the sight of her delicate hands spreading lotion all over her heavenly thighs make me squirm.

Emily continued with her evening routine, flaunting her nakedness before me like I was a dog. She spread foundation on her face and brushed in a light layer of blush. She scrunched her face up in the mirror and scrutinized herself. She dabbed creams into missing spots. She pursed her lips into the mirror and applied a bright red lipstick to her lips. They glistened like fresh fruit in the mirror. All the while she hummed to herself like she was alone with hours to spare. And all the while I watched helplessly, too frustrated to even speak.

When she finally finished her routine, she shot me a sudden glance that startled me. Her stare was severe and vaguely threatening. But then her gaze softened and a tiny smile played on her painted lips. "You're being such a good boy," she cooed. "Are you ready to get dressed?"

She walked over to me and started untying my hands. Her bare skin radiated heat inches from my face. The fresh scent of her body tantalized me. When she finally released my hands, they dropped limply to my sides. I could barely lift them. Pins and needles jabbed them from my shoulders to my wrists. I struggled to rise on my aching knees.

"Aw, poor boy," she said, seeing my predicament. She leaned forward and cupped me under the armpits, helping me to my feet. I rose clumsily until I was standing right in front of her. Her face was expertly made up, full and lush and vibrant without overdoing it. Her hair was silky soft and swept back, cascading down her naked shoulders.

I couldn't help but run my eyes all over her body. I wanted to touch her so badly, but I knew I would just get smacked if I did. Our closeness had my cock swelling up again, hanging heavily between my legs. She smirked down at it.

"Ok, dirty boy," she said. She reached down and took my cock in her hand. Her touch made me jump. "Let's get you dressed up for our date." She gave my cock a firm tug, forcing me to take a step forward to stop her from hurting it. And that's how she led me through the cabin, pulling me by my cock like a dog on a leash. I waddled after her, struggling to keep up and save myself from a painful jerk.

She tugged me into the bedroom and pulled me over to the bed. Then she gave me a look up and down. The twinkling mischief was in her eyes again. My heart pounded. *What now?*

"I can't stop thinking about what that ranger said," she told me. "When he asked if those panties were yours. Wasn't that so funny?"

I swallowed hard and nodded, trying to pretend I didn't know exactly where this was going. Emily smiled sweetly at me. "So funny," she repeated. She dug through her luggage and pulled out a tiny pair of pink panties with a frilly fringe all around the edges. "Aren't these cute?"

I pictured her slipping them up her thighs and nestling them around her butt. My cock twitched. "So cute," I murmured.

She displayed them in front of her, holding them with her thumbs so that they covered her crotch. "I brought them to wear tonight," she said. "I thought you might like knowing I had them on underneath my dress."

"I love that."

Emily's eyes traveled down my body. "But now," she said, pursing her lips. "Now, I can't stop picturing *you* wearing them."

My stomach ached. "Emily-" I stammered. "Please-"

"Aw, poor puppy," she smiled at me. "You don't have to wear them if you don't want to." Her eyes twinkled. "Unless you want to cum tonight."

My heart was pounding in my chest. "But I-" I

started, but she silenced me with a finger.

"It's your choice," she told me. "I wear these panties, and you spend all night picturing them on me and getting frustrated. Or *you* wear them, and I take care of you when we get back here."

There was no choice to be made. There was no way I could go the rest of the night without release. My cock still throbbed painfully against my thigh, desperate to cum. Without a word, I reached out and took the soft pink panties in my hand.

Emily squealed with delight at my choice. "Good boy!" She ran her tongue over her painted lips. "Now, let's see them on you."

Cheeks burning with shame, I stepped into the panties. They stretched slightly as I pulled them over my thighs, but I managed to pull them up to my waist until they were firm around me. The soft fabric cupped my heavy cock and balls up against me and tugged my butt up. There was a strange comfort to the way they held my delicate bits tight to me.

Emily stared at me with a predatory hunger. I expected giggles and laughter, but the look she gave me made me worry she would eat me alive. "Turn around," she said. I obeyed, turning to let her inspect how the panties shaped my ass. "Look at that *peach*," she growled, and she landed a stinging slap on my butt that made me jump. "You've got the ass of a Brazilian gymnast. I've never seen anything like it on a guy before."

I turned back, shame-faced, my hands darting down to cover my package. "Poor boy," Emily cackled. She reached down and gave one of the pubic hairs poking out from the panties a hard tug. "I should have made you shave," she said. "Well, there's always next time."

Next time? I couldn't believe I was going along with any of this. I'd expected to spend the weekend fucking Emily as many times as I could. Not standing in front of her in a pair of lacy panties while she talked about shaving me. And why was my dick so hard? It was all her fault. She'd gotten me so frustrated that I was willing to do anything for my release. Even be humiliated like this. But there was no denying how turned on I was.

143

Emily rummaged in her bag for some more clothes. She found a lacy pink bra that matched the panties she'd given me, and fastened it around her chest. It tugged her small ripe breasts together, creating a neat line of cleavage. My cock throbbed. "I was going to wear them as a set," she said, fishing around her luggage again. "But I guess I'll have to go without any panties."

She grinned at me. "Don't you like the sound of that?" I did. The thought of her bare smooth pussy just beneath the dress made me salivate. She pulled a soft cotton dress over her head and tugged it past her waist. The dress had a funky, vintage vibe that was playful but sexy. Puffy short sleeves curved down into a deep neckline that revealed the curves of her breasts. The hemline dangled teasingly just below the midpoint of her thighs. She cinched the waist in with a chunky belt, showing off her slender waist.

"Last thing," she said, digging around the bag again for a pair of fishnet stockings. She cocked her leg up against the bedside table and wiggled the stocking over her dainty foot. Watching her slowly pull the stocking over her calves, up past her knees and to the center of her smooth thighs was torture. My cock struggled against the panties constricting it to my waist. Emily teased the other stocking up her leg, delighting in my obvious frustration.

When she was finished, she admired herself in the mirror. "What do you think?" she asked, giving a little twirl that whirled her skirt out like a pinwheel. I stared at her. She looked-

"Beautiful," I breathed. And she was. Her makeup accentuated her gorgeous features, and her blonde hair looked soft as silk in its tumbles around her throat. The dress was perfect mountain-town chic, funky yet sexy and fitted perfectly to her lithe body. Its teasing hemline and the fishnet stockings, combined with the bright red lipstick, hinted at a girl with a wild side. I couldn't believe someone who looked like her was going out with *me*. "You look incredible," I told her. "I can't believe you're my girlfriend."

She broke character and gave me a sweet smile. "I'm so happy to be here. I'm having so much fun with you," she told me. Then her face resumed its imperious command. "Hurry up and get dressed."

I scrambled over to my bag and started pulling out my clothes. "I can't believe I'm waiting on you to get ready," she teased. "Which one of us is the girl?"

I tried to shape a comeback about how she'd kept me waiting, but something about wearing a pair of pink panties in front of her made it difficult to defend my masculinity. I found a nicer pair of jeans and the flannel button-down I'd packed for our night out. They seemed perfect at the time I packed them, but seeing her dolled up in that dress and stockings made me realize she would be far more dressed up than me. I pulled the flannel shirt on and buttoned it under her scrutinizing gaze. But before I pulled me pants on, she commanded me to stop.

"What is it?" I asked.

Emily fought a smile spreading across her face. Something was going on in her mind. Some new level of depravity. The thought thrilled and terrified me. "I had a thought," she said. "Something to keep you extra frustrated all night."

My cock throbbed through the panties. "I don't think I can get anymore frustrated," I told her. "I already feel like I'm right on the edge."

"Come on, baby," she purred in a low, throaty voice. She strode over to me, her eyes filled with hunger. I was rooted to the spot in fear. She drew her face close to mine. I thought she was about to kiss me, but she stopped just inches from my lips. "I think it's so hot that you're right on the edge," she whispered to me. Her fingers brushed against my cock, and a trembling shiver ran through my body. "I'm going to love knowing how turned on and frustrated you are all night."

I tried to bring my lips to hers for a kiss, but she caught my face in her hand. "Don't you want to take this to the next level?" she asked.

There was no refusing her. Her glowing snake's eyes had me hypnotized. I would have done anything for her in that moment. I couldn't even speak. I just nodded mutely, turning my face over to her.

Emily laughed and flounced away from me. She bent down in front of her luggage, shamelessly displaying her full peach butt straining through her dress. I was practically drooling imagining sliding the skirt over her ass and sliding my desperate cock inside her bare pussy. When she found what she was looking for, she whirled around and displayed it to me. It took me a second to realize what was in her hand.

Oh god. She was holding a fat silicone buttplug. Her face was a malevolent smirk. "I brought this for me," she said, wiggling it around. "But just like those panties, I think it would be more fun if *you* wore it."

I was completely lost for words. "I don't-" I stammered, but she held up a hand to quiet me.

"Come on," she cajoled in a singsong voice. She moved toward me, brandishing the buttplug like a blade. "I bet it'll feel so good, pressing up there inside of you." Her head was cocked coyly to the side as she handed the plug out to me.

"I don't know," I said. The plug was so thick and

intimidating, wobbling in her hand like a sausage.

"Oh, pleeease-" Emily cooed. Her voice was irresistible. "It'll be so hot, eating dinner with you and knowing you've got this plug up your cute butt." She reached around me and gave my ass a firm slap that made me yelp. She fixed the full power of her shining eyes on me, just inches away from me. "Please, won't you do it for me?"

I should have known there was no resisting. I reached out and allowed her to put the plug in my hand. It was much heavier in my hand than I would have thought, but the material was spongy and yielding. Emily's happy giggle made me look away in shame. "Oh, good boy," she laughed. She leaned forward and gave me a quick peck on the cheek. Her hot lips made me shiver. "Now wait here a minute."

Once again she danced away, leaving me standing there in the button down shirt and the pink panties, holding the buttplug out like it was a grenade. She retrieved a small bottle of lube and rushed back to me. "Ok," she said, handing me the bottle. "Do I need to show you how to do it?"

"I can do it," I grumbled, my cheeks burning.

"Use a ton of it!" she said. "I want it to slide in nice and easy."

"Ok, ok," I said.

I started retreating to the bathroom, but she seized me by the flannel shirt. "Where do you think you're going?"

"Come on," I begged. "Give me some privacy for this."

Emily pursed her lips at me. "Fine," she said. "Let me tell you how to do it. Lay on your side. Pull those pretty panties down-" she gave me another firm slap on the rump- "and get this thing nice and lubed up. Spread some lube on your butt too. Then slowly push it inside you." She winked at me. "That's how I do it, anyway. If you're having trouble- just picture me doing it. Pretend you're me, laying there on the floor, working this plug up my butt. It'll help you."

The image of her slipping a buttplug into her perfect butt sent another twinge through my cock, and I felt myself stiffening again. "Got it."

I tried to slink away, but she caught me by the shirt again. She jerked me around and toward her, and I was shocked by the intensity burning in her eyes. "One more thing," she said in a threatening tone.

"What?" I stammered.

The intensity softened back into that teasing smirk, and her mischievous eyes glittered at me. She shot out her hand and gave my cock a sudden firm squeeze. "Don't you dare touch this dick while you're in there."

IX

"How are you doing, sweet boy?" Emily whispered, her fingers teasing against my inner thigh. It was hard to hear her over the din inside the brewpub where we'd ended up for dinner. A cavernous place called

Wicked Weed. Long tables packed with young and happy people, laughing and talking and eating and drinking up a storm. It was a perfect crisp and clear autumn evening outside, and the town was just starting to stir. There was a promise in the air and in the strange faces that surrounded us.

In my jeans and flannel, I fit in with the general look of the people surrounding us. But Emily stood out from the crowd. Her fishnets and short dress drew stares from men and women when we walked in, and I noticed several girlfriends slapping their boyfriends' shoulders to scold them for blatantly checking her out. I was somewhat used to the attention she got whenever we went out, but this was a new level. Even I couldn't stop staring at her. Her slender body and gorgeous face constantly distracted me, and she took great delight in torturing me with all her assets.

As I stared at her from our seats at the table, my cock struggled against the pink panties she had forced me to wear. The constant pressure from the thick plug inside me curled up my toes and forced my fingers into tight fists. Every bump along our drive down the mountainside had forced the buttplug deeper inside me, sending shocking jolts through my body. I'd never had anything inside my butt before, and I couldn't believe how intense the sensation against my prostate was. It seemed to push out a constant wetness from the end of my cock. At times I felt like it would be too much and I would explode just from the sensation of my dick rubbing against the panties.

"I'm hanging in there," I told Emily.

Beneath the table, Emily's fingers drifted over to my cock. It twitched and strained inside my pants. "Oh my god," she said, stifling a giggle. "You're still so hard."

"Everything alright here?" asked a waiter who had materialized behind us.

I jumped. I expected Emily to jerk her hand away, but she kept it wedged just inside my inner thigh. "Yes, sir!" she said. She pinched my thigh hard with one hand and held up the menu with the other. "I'd like the Golden Angel Sour, please."

"Excellent choice," said the waiter. He was your

classic Asheville guy- white with dreadlocks that hung down to the center of his back, and a thick fuzz around his face. He was probably saving cash for his Appalachian Trail thru-hike. I noticed his eyes linger on Emily's chest before they flickered over to me. "And for you?"

"Um," I mumbled, picking up the menu. Emily leaned over, pretending to help. But beneath the table, she was making my decision process even harder. She slid her hand from my thighs and wedged it underneath my butt. I felt her fingers crawl around, searching, until they found the base of the plug inside me. "I think I'll have the-" I gave a sudden yelp as Emily pressed the base of the plug hard, forcing it up against my prostate. My cock throbbed from the sudden wave of sensation emanating from deep inside me.

I cleared my throat and tried not to wither beneath the waiter's smirk. "I'll have the Pernicious IPA."

"And I think we're ready to order," Emily broke in. She pressed the plug hard again, forcing me to squirm in my seat. She flashed a wide smile at the waiter. "I'm *so* hungry."

The waiter returned the smile, and his eyes blatantly traveled down her fishnet stockings. "What can I get for you?"

"The New York Strip," Emily said without hesitation. "Rare."

"Excellent," said the waiter. He looked to me with barely concealed disdain. "You?"

Emily worked her fingers in a rhythm, forcing the plug in and out of me. My cock was achingly hard in my pants. I could swear it was leaking cum. "I'll have the bison burger-" I gasped. A deep thrust made me seize the tablecloth to keep from crying out. The nonplussed waiter watched bemused as I struggled to compose myself. "Bison burger," I repeated. "Medium."

"Very well," said the confused waiter, and he disappeared. Emily giggled and pressed the plug deep into me again.

I felt a warm yearning pressure inside me, and

realized I was getting close to danger. "Careful," I warned. "I'm right there. I feel like I could cum any second."

"You better not, dirty boy," scolded Emily, pulling her hand away. She clicked her tongue. "Getting off with a buttplug in your ass. You're such a little pervert, do you know that?"

I nodded meekly, unable to respond. I couldn't believe it either. Just a day before, the thought of putting something in my ass would have been a joke to me. Yet here I was, practically drooling from the sensation of the plug forcing itself against that nut of pleasure hidden deep inside me.

Emily tickled my inner thigh again. "I love that," she said in a confessional tone. "I'm having so much fun with you."

"Me too," I admitted.

"You're really that close?" Her fingers drifted dangerously close again.

I tried to ignore the pulsating sensation in my cock. "I swear, it would take almost nothing to put me over the edge."

Emily's voice took on her domineering tone again. "Next time I'll have to lock that thing up," she warned. "You know they make little cages for boys like you who can't control themselves."

I shuddered at the thought of my penis being constricted. I imagined some kind of medieval torture device crushing down on me. But Emily went on in a seductive tone. "Can you imagine that, baby?" she purred. "Your dick locked up, and me holding the key. You constantly frustrated. So desperately horny for your release that you'd do *anything* for me to let you cum?"

I couldn't believe the effect her words had on me. The concept terrified me, but her erotic voice and the teasing touch on my thigh had me aching for more. I started to speak, but she stopped me with a finger to my lips. Her eyes were smouldering. "I think it would be so hot," she said. "I could make you my own personal slave. Make you earn every orgasm. Oh, I'd have your sweet face between my legs every day," she said, pressing her finger inside my lips.

I gave her finger a playful bite. "What's in it for me?"

Her eyes flashed. "Oh, there's plenty in it for you," she said. "You remember how good it felt when I finally let you cum last night?"

I remembered the couch in the cabin, my hands tied behind my back, Emily in my lap, her fingers inside herself, her knuckles just brushing against my cock until I exploded. The intensity of that orgam was unlike any I'd experienced before, even though she was barely touching my cock. "That did feel amazing," I admitted.

"And that was just after one day," Emily told me. "Imagine if I built you up for a couple days straight." She arched her back in her chair, displaying her chest to me. She wielded the seductive power she held over me with utter confidence. "Imagine if I kept you teased and frustrated and just dying for that release. How much better it would feel than just a quick jerk-off. That anticipation would make it so worth it. And when I finally let you cum, you'd shoot such a massive load... I bet it would feel incredible."

Her tantalizing touch had me shivering. "That does sound amazing," I told her softly.

She flashed that warm sweet smile and gently stroked my cheek. "Good boy," she said. "I'm going to enjoy turning you into my sweet little pet. We're going to have so much fun together."

The waiter rematerialized behind us, his face contorted in a resentful sneer at the sight of Emily touching my cheek. I noticed him help himself to another eyeful of her body as he set down our drinks. "Enjoy," he said. "Your food will be out in a minute."

Emily lifted her glass in the air. "Here's to us," she said. There was lovingkindness in her eyes again. A softness behind the mask of teasing cruelty she'd worn all weekend. "And to this amazing weekend."

I locked my eyes with hers. All her words raced in

159

my mind. Tantalizing promises of a life we could have together. It all seemed so strange and frightening, but desperately alluring to me. And in her sweet loving eyes and smile, I found a depth of trust that let me know that it was safe to let go and give myself over to these fantasies. And give myself to her. To my surprise, sentimental tears stung my eyes. Emily was so beautiful in her dress beside me. And her expression of sweetness and love enveloped me tighter than a hug. *It will all be ok, as long as I have her.* I raised my beer. "And to our future."

X

We each enjoyed a couple beers with dinner and left the brewery slightly tipsy. I held her hand tight as we explored the hilly streets of Asheville, looking for our next spot. The aching hunger for Emily still gnawed at me, and deep down all I wanted was to head back to our cabin and make love to her until dawn. But the night was young, the moon was full, and the streets brimmed with lively promise. Besides- Emily was in the mood for some fun.

We raced hand in hand down the streets, peering into all the bars and restaurants and imagining what we might find inside. Her giddiness sent my heart racing. She radiated an infectious energy. I felt like we were being pulled along by an invisible cord, floating toward our unknown destination. There was a joy in our letting go. And even the keen hunger for her spurred me on. My thoughts were dulled. I simply reacted. I had never before been so caught up in the moment as I felt racing down that moonlit mountain street with Emily on that chilly autumn night, surrounded by a thousand strangers.

The evening's current swept us through the brewing district, past dozens of packed bars and breweries. An impulse took us down a side-street, heading toward a brightly lit park. The sidestreet was dark and secluded, almost an alley. Within just a few feet, the noise of the crowds died away and we could hear our footsteps in the dark. It was a world different than the crowded street we'd just left. Emily took my hand and led me down the dark street toward the park in the distance.

We were halfway to the next intersection when Emily halted in front of a dark storefront. "Oooh, look!"

she cried. The storefront was built into the first floor of a shabby concrete multistory that slouched in the alley like a wino. It was dark, with heavy curtains blocking any view through the windows. It would have looked closed if it weren't for the two lit-up neon signs in the heavily curtained windows. The larger sign glowed above the door in flourishing script that read NANCY'S NOOK. The other neon sign simply read ADULTS ONLY. In the dark evening chill, the place had an eerie aura.

Emily didn't seem disturbed at all. "What do you think it is?" she asked.

"I don't know." Something about the building unnerved me. Its shadowed darkness, the closed curtains, the strange neon glow from the simple signs. It was hardly inviting. I wanted to pull away, but Emily seemed transfixed by it. "Probably a head shop."

"I bet it's a sex shop," said Emily.

"It looks closed," I said. I glanced down the street. Something about the building made me want to break into a full sprint to get away. But I could feel it drawing Emily in.

"Should we try the door?" she asked.

"I don't know…"

Emily poked me playfully in the ribs. "Come on, you big girl," she teased. "You're taking this 'wearing panties' thing a little too seriously."

My cock twitched inside the pink panties that bound it. "Fine," I said. I tried to look confident walking to the door, but I was sure Emily could see right through the anxiety I felt. And I was sure she loved it. I approached the heavy door and gripped the knob, praying I would find it locked. But to my surprise, it popped open.

Inside was a small shop lit by red lights and lava lamps. Glass cases encircled racks of clothes and other items, and the walls were draped in brightly colored posters. A stupefying haze of incense hung heavy in the air. It was warm inside, cozy and slightly stuffy, and enticing compared to the bracing wind on the street.

I stood in the doorway, peering into the store, until Emily prodded me in the back. "Hurry up," she said, "I'm freezing out here!"

She followed me into the hazy dark store. At first glance I was sure my guess that it was a head shop was right, until I realized that the glass cases were filled with dildoes and other toys. The posters on the walls were strangely erotic art

"See?" Emily whispered. "It is a sex shop!"

A voice from behind startled both of us. "Can I help you find something?"

Behind the counter was a young woman with a punk-rock look to her. She was heavy-set; sturdy but not fat. The sides of her head were shaved, and the mop of hair on top of her head was dyed blue and combed aggressively to the side. Her leather jacket was lined with intimidating metal studs, similar to the ones that porcupined her ears, lips, and nose.

"Are you Nancy?" Emily asked.

The girl's lip curled up in a smirk. "Yes, I am," she said. She swept her hand around the store. "Welcome to my little nook."

"It's so cool," Emily gushed. I tried to avoid getting caught looking at anything, and kept my gaze on the ceiling.

"Thanks," said Nancy. She was eyeing Emily up and down even more than the Wicked Weed waiter. "What are you looking for today, doll?"

"Oh, nothing in particular," Emily laughed. She squeezed my hand. "Maybe something fun for me and my boyfriend here."

Nancy's eyes flickered over to me. "Well, we've got all the costumes and toys you could want," she told Emily. "Just let me know if you need a hand with anything." She looked back down at the magazine spread out in front of her on the counter.

"Actually," Emily began. Her tone let me know

she in the mood to make trouble. She shot me a quick smile. "There is something you could help me with. Do you carry chastity cages here?"

Nancy's head shot up from the magazine. She fought to control the slow smile spreading over her face, and gave me a long deliberate look with mirth glimmering in her eyes. My cheeks were flushed completely red. I wanted to melt into the ground and hide my face. I'd never been so embarrassed before in my life. The thought of this girl knowing our secret, knowing my penis would be locked away, was humiliating beyond belief.

"So…" Nancy said in a drawn-out, teasing tone. "Looking for some control over your bad boy, huh?"

"He needs it," Emily answered, matching Nancy's tone. She gave me a playful squeeze on the butt. "He can't keep his hands to himself. Or *off* himself."

"I don't-" I started, but Nancy was already circling around the counter.

"Follow," she ordered. Emily pulled me along

behind her, leading me past racks of latex outfits and bondage gear. I tried to avert my eyes from the intimidating dildoes and plugs arrayed in cases around the room. All of them seemed to be pointing directly at me. With each step, the butt plug forced itself against my prostate, weakening my knees.

Nancy led us to a glass case near a set of wooden dressing room doors. The case was lined with an assortment of small cages. They were made from different materials- some metal, some plastic- but each had the same distinctive cylindrical shape. "We have all types of cages," Nancy said, gesturing inside the case. Her words were addressed only to Emily; she wouldn't even look at me.

"I'm not sure I-" I started, but Emily cut me off with a harsh stare.

"Quiet," she hissed, her eyes narrowed. "No speaking unless spoken to."

Nancy nodded with approval at this scolding. "Very good," she said. She pushed back the case's heavy glass lid and reached inside. The first device she held up was made of clear plastic. It consisted of an open circular band and a penis-shaped sheath, with a small padlock on the top. "This is our most basic unit," Nancy explained. She tapped her fingernail on the cage. A hollow, plastic echo sounded, and a shiver went down my spine.

Emily took the cage from Nancy and furrowed her brow at it. "How does he pee?"

Nancy's smirk flashed over to me for a half second before she turned back to Emily. "He'll have to sit down." She flicked her eyes over to me again. "Like a girl."

Emily giggled. She suddenly thrust her hand out to me, holding the cage out right in front of my crotch. I flinched, fearing she was about to hit me, but she didn't touch me. The cage hovered just inches from me. Emily gave me that mischievous smile. "What do you think?"

I examined the plastic cage she held in front of me, trying to imagine squeezing my cock inside it. "It's so small."

Emily and Nancy both giggled at this comment. "Don't give yourself too much credit," said Emily. She said it with a wink that made me think she must be joking. *I hope she's joking.*

Nancy cleared her throat. "Most men are growers," she said. She had the calm, detached tone of someone discussing a science fact they'd heard. "As long as you put it on while you are flaccid, the device will restrict any growth in that area."

This sent Emily into another fit of laughter. "Poor boy," she teased. "All locked away. You won't even be able to touch it."

"We have a variety of other, more advanced models, if you'd like," Nancy said. She displayed an intimidating metal instrument consisting of metal coils wrapped in a tight, narrow tube. Its cold gleam made me shudder.

Emily dismissed this option with a wave of her hand. "Maybe someday," she said. "But for now, I think we'll start with something basic."

"Very well," said Nancy. She replaced the metal cage and closed the lid. "So, you'd like to purchase the basic model?"

"Yes, please." We followed Nancy back through the forest of dildoes and bondage gear to the register. Nancy rang up the purchase and swiped Emily's debit card.

"Thank you so much," said Nancy. She winked at me. "Enjoy."

I reached for the bag, desperate to scurry out of the store. *Finally*, I thought, *at least we're almost out of here.*

But Emily stopped me. She stared absently into space, clearly playing with some devious plan in her mind. "Excuse me," she said to Nancy. "But do you have a dressing room here? I think my boy is excited to try out our new purchase."

I swallowed hard. *I knew this wasn't over.* Nancy raised her eyebrows at us. "*Really?*" she said with surprise. "Well, then. If you can't wait," she said with another wink at me. My stomach burned with shame. "Feel free to go to the dressing rooms to the back."

Emily grabbed my hand and started pulling me to the back of the store. "Thank you!"

"I usually don't let couples in there together," Nancy called across the store as Emily pulled me to the back. "Because I don't want people getting frisky in there. But in this case, I guess the opposite is going to happen!"

The dressing room was warm and close. Emily stood right next to me, holding the small plastic cage. She smelled like autumn and alcohol, and her eyes radiated a passionate intensity. She was standing so close I could feel the heat from her skin.

"This is so much fun," she whispered. I found myself nodding at her, shocked that I felt the same way. Despite the humiliation from Nancy, I didn't want to stop. Emily's enthusiasm was infectious, and my frustration was so keen. All I wanted to do was please her.

She removed the small padlock from the cage and handed its components to me. I set them on the table and unzipped my pants, showing a flash of the pink panties. Then I stopped. Emily shook my shoulder. "Come on," she said. "What are you waiting for?"

But there was an obvious problem to me "It's not going to fit," I said, tugging down my jeans a little more. My cock was swollen up, bulging hard against the grip of Emily's soft pink panties. There was no way I could stuff it inside that small plastic sheath.

Emily giggled at my predicament. "Oh, my," she said, covering her mouth. She thought for a moment.
"How do we get it to go down?"

"I don't know," I said. "Usually I have to… you know…"

Emily folded her arms. "Cum?" she said, arching her eyebrow like an angry headmistress. "Out of the question." She squeezed her lips together, deep in thought.

"Then how do I…"

"Shh!" Emily hissed. "I'm thinking." I stood in silence, my cock throbbing against the pink panties, the buttplug pulsating in my ass, my cheeks flushed with shame, while Emily considered the problem. Then she perked up. "I have an idea," she said. She scooped up the chastity cage components and grabbed me by the arm. "Come on."

Once again I found myself being tugged through the sex shop as the butt plug worked itself inside me. I barely had time to pull my jeans up to cover my shame before we appeared in front of Nancy again. "Is there a back door here?" Emily asked her. "We've got a little bit of a problem here, and I think mother nature might be able to help us take care of it."

Nancy matched Emily's evil grin. "No backdoor, I'm afraid," she said with a shrug. "But I think I know what you have in mind. Feel free to just use the front step. If anyone sees you… well, I'll just take it as an advertisement for our services."

The next thing I knew, Emily was dragging me

173

back to the entrance. She whipped the front door open. A blast of cold autumn air whipped inside, chilling me to the bone. Emily prodded me from behind. "Go on," she said, like I was an indecisive dog. "Get out there."

I found myself on the store's front stoop, my hands clutched tight to me. Emily followed after. The chilly air seemed to intensify her excitement. It had the opposite effect on me.

"Come on," she said, looking down at my pants. "Pull it out."

My eyes darted around the dark alley. There was nobody around, but I still felt fully exposed to any prying eyes. I slowly tugged down my jeans, and the cold air prickled against my bare thighs and whipped through the thin panties. I gave another glance around to make sure nobody was coming. And then, I tugged the pink panties down and let my cock flop out.

My penis seemed to feel the same way about the chilly wind and the exposure as the rest of me did. It shrank up inside itself like a frightened turtle, despite the frustration that had built inside it. Emily was nearly doubled over laughing at the sight of its rapid reduction.

"Look at that!" she giggled, swatting away my hands that tried to cover it. "It looks tiny!"

"Just give me the cage," I groaned, trying to hide from her. She handed the parts to me, and I slipped the circular component underneath my shriveled testicles. It nestled against the tip of my taint, gently constricting the base of my cock and balls in a horseshoe-like vise. The sheath was a little trickier, given the chilly air, but I managed to wiggle my penis inside it. I was almost grateful for the protection it provided my limp cock against the night air.

When I'd worked my cock all the way inside and snapped the device shut, I turned to Emily. "Ok," I said through chattering teeth. "Done."

"Not yet!" she said. She held up the small padlock. "We've got to do the most important part."

"I can do it," I stammered, reaching for the lock,

but she dodged my grasping hands. I gasped in shock as she seized my cock and balls around the base in a firm grip. I felt a rush of blood in my cock from the warmth of her hand, but the cold plastic restricted me to a strange pulsing sensation.

With deft fingers, Emily worked the padlock through the little eyelet and locked it shut. "Ta-dah," she said, stepping back to admire her handiwork.

I peered down into the darkness past my waist and gasped at what I saw. The clear plastic cage glinted in the faint neon storefront lights. My cock was fully constricted in the tiny plastic device that wrapped around the base of my balls and over the head of my dick. Tingles of evening breeze whipped around my exposed skin. "It's so…"

"Tiny!" Emily said. She grabbed the plastic cage in her hand. I couldn't feel her touch on my dick, but only the light tugging from the base of my balls. "Oh my god, look at you!"

"Ok, ok," I said, reaching for my pants. "It's freezing out here!" I snugged up the soft pink panties over the cage. It tucked into them nicely, creating a firm bulge in the cotton. Then I zipped up my jeans.

"How's it feel?" Emily asked.

"Strange," I admitted. "Really tight." I shivered, and gave her a plaintive look. "Can we go, please? I'm freezing."

"Hold on," said Emily. "We have to say goodbye to Nancy!"

"Oh, god," I groaned, but it was too late. Emily was already pulling me back inside the sex shop. At least it was warm inside the building. The stale, incense-laden air sent blood tingling through my fingers and face again.

Nancy waited for us with her arms folded and a smirk playing on her pierced lips. "Well?" she asked, raising her eyebrows at me. "Success?"

"Oh, yes," said Emily. She held the cage key aloft like a trophy. "He's not going to have any fun without my permission."

I angled my hips away from Nancy, as if somehow she could see through my jeans and know my shameful secret. *At least we can go home now,* I thought.

"You know," Nancy began. She looked around the empty sex shop as if making sure nobody was around. Then she leaned forward with a conspiratorial whisper. "There's a place for people with similar… interests," she said.

Emily's eyes shot open. "Really?"

"Oh, yes," Nancy continued. "It's a private club. Not too far from here. I can give you the password, if you're looking for some more fun tonight."

Emily squeezed my hand and fixed me with her big, sweet eyes. "What do you think?" she asked. "One more stop?"

My stomach clenched tight. The night had already been such a chaotic whirlwind. So much of me just wanted to retreat back to the cabin with Emily. But we were being swept along by the evening, carried along on this wild journey. And in my frustrated state I was hardly going to be able to resist her charms. "I don't know-" I said weakly.

"Just one drink," Emily cooed. She squeezed my hand again, and waved the padlock key teasingly in front of me. "I promise, I'll make it worth your while."

The lewd promise in her voice sent a rush of blood to my cock. It started to swell, but was constrained by the tight plastic sheath. A weird, yearning pulse ran through my body, centered at the base of my cock. This throbbing was magnified by the pressure from the butt plug inside me, until it felt like I was being slowly squeezed to death in the belly of a charming serpent. I was desperate for relief. And Emily was the only way I was going to get it. I nodded at her. "Ok," I murmured. "One drink."

Nancy was already scribbling down directions for us. "You'll love it," she said, handing the scrap of paper to Emily. Then she fixed us with a serious look. "Just be ready. Things can get a little wild there."

XI

Nancy's directions led us down a maze of side streets. Ever step took us further from the sounds of revelry on the main drag of town. We walked in eerie silence through the alleys, clinging close together in the dark. Nobody was around. The chilly autumn wind whipped through us, and we had to squint in the dark to see the street signs.

And all along the way, I felt the constriction of my chastity and the pressure of the plug working itself inside me with every step, all bound up in the soft tight cotton panties that constricted me. It was such a strange feeling to have all that hidden underneath my clothes. At least nobody was around to see me.

Emily led us through the dark. She kept a firm grip on my hand, pulling me along like a puppy. We didn't speak; she was too focused on leading us to our destination. Her excitement was palpable and infectious. As exhausted and frustrated as I was, I let her carry us along into the evening.

We reached a dark multistory building on the edge of an alley. A stairwell led down to a baroque wooden door with thick brass knockers and a gilded fringe around it. The door was lit by two electric lights shaped like torches on either side. It was utterly incongruous in this setting on the street, looking more appropriate for a medieval city than the basement floor of a dilapidated building.

Emily tugged me toward the stairs. "This must be it. Come on."

I tried to ignore the nervous spasms in my stomach as we descended toward the door. The vague thump of electric bass vibrated through the door. Emily shared none of my trepidation. She marched straight to the door and rapped it with her knuckles.

A panel slid open, but all we could see through it was a tiny dark rectangle. Through this hole, a deep male voice called out. "Password?"

Emily squinted at the paper in the faint light. "*Roquelaure.*"

The panel slammed shut. There was a brief silence. I turned to Emily, expecting we would be barred from entry and getting ready to suggest we leave. But then, there was the sound of a turning lock. A scrape and a rasp. And then, the heavy door swung open.
Immediately the thump-thump of the music grew louder, echoing down a long, narrow corridor lit by blood-red fluorescence. A linebacker-sized man in a suit vest filled the door frame momentarily. He inspected us coldly, eyes running over our bodies. His officious gaze and fancy attire made me feel under-dressed in my simple outfit.

Apparently the bouncer saw enough. He stepped aside and allowed us to enter. As soon as we were past him, he let the heavy door slam behind us. Wordlessly, he took our coats from us. Emily slid her coat from her shoulders, once again revealing her incredible body beneath the dress. I remembered that she wasn't wearing panties underneath that dress, and I felt a stirring inside me. I cursed the device that kept me constricted and handed over my jacket.

The bouncer pointed us down the blood-red corridor, which was lit up like an air raid shelter. The throbbing jungle music was dampened by the stone walls, but we could tell it was close. I pocketed our coat-check tickets and allowed Emily to lead us down the hallway toward the music.

The music grew louder as we headed down the eerie corridor. As we approached the curtain at the end, we could hear the faint sound of human voices mixing in with the heavy music throb. We drew nearer, neither of us knowing what we faced on the other side of the curtain.

Emily squeezed my hand. "Ready?" I nodded. She smiled and pulled aside the curtain.

On the other side of the curtain was a crowded bar, bumping with hypnotic music and loud voices. Playful shouts and laughter echoed over the throbbing base din. The bar was chic, filled with onyx tables arrayed with empty glasses. On the far side of the room, a pair of tuxedoed bartenders waited on the pressed-in revelers, shaking mixers to the beat of the music.

As our eyes adjusted to the fluorescent light, the crowd of patrons in the bar became clearer to me. They were dressed in a wild assortment of costumes, ranging from upscale cocktail attire to shockingly skimpy fetish attire. Some of the women were almost entirely nude save for thin strips of leather and lace wrapped around their most delicate areas. And on further examination, some of the men were clad in just as little.

There was also a wide assortment of costumes and masks. A winged angel in a tiny skirt gyrated in the arms of a lion. Marie Antoinette and the devil kissed passionately in a secluded corner. A ballerina led a hulking male bodybuilder around on a leash. To my surprise, there was a good smattering of men dressed in ultra-feminine skirts and stockings, and many women in macho drag as well. In the flashing lights and crowded chaos, there were many figures who blurred the gender lines beyond the point of identification. And the somehow the strangest part was the many distinguished-looking attendees, incongruous in their formal eveningwear, seemed utterly indifferent to their madcap surroundings.

I squeezed Emily's hand. "Where are we?" I whispered *sotto voce* over the din of the music.

Emily squeezed me back. "It must be some kind of swinger club," she guessed. She jabbed her finger in the corner, where two women in pixie outfits were kissing fiercely under the approving eye of a Peter Pan and a Captain Hook. "Look at them!"

I gestured past them to another couple- a petite schoolgirl with a thick beard gyrating with a slender man in an old-timey naval uniform. "Look at *them!*"

"You'd look good in that," Emily winked. She cocked her head over at the bar. "Buy me a drink?"

We weaved our way through the strange carnival. The mass of bodies jostled us along the way. The air was heavy with perfume and leather and desire, all pulsing under the lights of this wild place. I had to stop myself from staring at so many of the people. Men, women, and everything in between all strutted and flirted and kissed openly, and constant laughter and cheers sounded over the din of the music.

Our bartender, a vested, Faustian figure with a pointed goatee, approached with a thin smile. I tried to order us two tequila sodas, but he held up an authoritative hand. "We don't do that here," he said. "There's only one thing on the menu." His eyes flashed over to someone I couldn't see, and he cocked his head toward us. *Who was he gesturing to?* I was about to ask, but he leaned behind the bar. When he stood, he served us two blood-red drinks in ornate glasses. I started to pull out my wallet but he waved me away. "First ones are free." I watched his eyes flicker back to the spot he had look before, and he indicated me and Emily with his head again.

We ferried our beverages away from the crowded bar, seeking a quieter place to sit and regroup. Past the mass of bodies dancing on the floor, we found a series of small booths draped with heavy curtains. We slid onto the cushioned seats, sitting next to each other so we could hear each other. The curtained booth was cozy and semiprivate, and drowned out the music enough for us to speak normally.

Emily cocked her eyebrow at me. "So, what do

you think?"

"This place is wild," I admitted.

Emily smiled sweetly. "I know it's a lot," she said. "Thanks for coming with me."

I lost myself in her sweet eyes, her heartbreaking smile, overwhelmed by the depth of my feelings for her. "I'd go anywhere with you."

She leaned forward and kissed me softly on the lips, a slow lingering kiss. Fire filled my belly. She stroked my cheek tenderly. Then she raised her glass. "Here's to us," she toasted.

We clinked glasses and sipped the red concoction that swirled inside. It was rich and tart but not cloying. It was the kind of refreshing sweet thirst-quencher you could drink all night. Her eyes glittered in the refracted light from her glass.

Just then, a deep voice interrupted us. "Enjoying yourselves?"

We turned, both of us slightly startled, to find a dapper man standing beside our booth. He was a burly man, broad and stocky, looking somewhere around forty years old. He had a neatly trimmed blonde beard and thick head of matching hair combed sharply to the side. He wore a crisp cream-colored button down shirt that strained against his broad chest. The sleeves were rolled up past his thick forearms. This shirt was tucked into a pair of black leather pants that gleamed in the semidark room.

"Uh, yes, we are," I answered, a little uncertain. *Who is this dude*?

He extended his hand to me, and I took it with some trepidation. "Stefan," he said, his powerful hand enveloping mine in a firm but warm embrace. "I host this little… gathering."

"Oh my goodness," said Emily, taking his hand after mine. "It's so nice to meet you. This place is amazing."

"First time here, I presume?"

"Yeah," I answered.

"But we're loving it!" Emily piped up.

Stefan observed us with a curious, unhurried expression. He did not appear a bit self-conscious about openly reviewing us with his eyes. I realized that we- or, at least, *I*- looked out of place among the glamorous and bizarre patrons of the bar. Emily might have been slightly underdressed, but was so gorgeous in her dress and fishnet stockings that it didn't matter. On the other hand, my flannel shirt and button down might have fit in in a mountain-town brewery, but made me look decidedly square among the crowd in this club. And what was worse- I could tell Stefan was reviewing us to figure out how we had gotten in there. I had the feeling invitations were difficult to come by.

Stefan showed a gentleman character by politely probing for details, rather than accusing us of gatecrashing. "I'm so glad to hear you're enjoying yourselves," he said. He continued observing us with curiosity, like we were aliens who had just come to earth.

"So, what brought you to my little get-together?"

Translation: How did a couple normies get through my door? I fidgeted, trying to think of a response, until Emily cut in. "We heard about it from Nancy," she explained. "You know, from-"

"Nancy's Nook," Stefan finished. He flashed a brief smile. "Yes, I know Nancy very well. Her store is fantastic. So… she gave you the password?"

"She did," Emily said.

"Interesting." Stefan stroked the beard on his chin thoughtfully. It was strange to be under his examination, although nothing about him seemed threatening. He pursed his lips. "Nancy is usually quite selective in who she sends my way.' He flashed an apologetic smile. "Forgive me," he said. "It's not that you aren't a handsome couple. But you must have done something else to impress her."

"Oh." I looked down, my cheeks flushing. *He's trying to figure out what we're into.* Suddenly I sensed the cage around my cock and the plug in my butt and the pink panties binding them all.

Emily also realized what Stefan was getting at. And of course she was eager to play along. "I guess she must have been impressed by what we were bought," she said. "And that one of us wore it out of the store."

Stefan's raised eyes showed his comprehension. "I see," he said, with a smile. He was clearly enjoying the game of trying to uncover our kinky secret. "Well, she does have many fine products for *everyone* to enjoy." He looked back and forth between us, trying to decide which of us hid a secret beneath our clothes. The answer must have been written all over me; I couldn't even look at him. My cheeks burned with shame.

He grasped me warmly by the shoulder, his eyes commanding me to raise my gaze. "Well, whatever it was, I'm sure you two made an impression," he said. He extended a powerful arm toward the club's interior. "Care for a tour of the place?"

Emily and I made only brief eye contact before she

started standing. I followed suit, feeling uneasy. Stefan seemed trustworthy and polite, a far cry from what I would expect from a sex club owner. His stare was intense, but not lewd. His behavior was respectable. But there was still a mysterious, intimidating charisma to this powerfully built man. I wasn't sure what to make of him. I almost said as much to Emily, but she was too far ahead of me, tagging along with Stefan as he led her past the dance floor.

Stefan indicated the mass of bodies crowded in the main bar room we'd passed through before, all pulsing together in their strange attire. "We try to keep it PG out here in the main room," Stefan explained. "Well, PG-13," he added with a wink.

"Lots of people come here with all kinds of different interests," he went on, guiding us by the bar. "Many of them don't want to sleep with anyone other than the person they came with. But they enjoy the charge they get from the atmosphere here." His face grew serious. "I don't tolerate aggressive behavior here," he said. "You can find that nonsense at any trashy bar you want. I'm striving for a fun but cultivated vibe. I believe people have a much easier time opening up and being their true selves when they don't feel pressure from anyone."

We headed down a corridor, and the club grew darker and more eerily lit. Rows of doorways lined the hallway, all covered with thick red curtains where they doors should have been. The music was quieter down in the corridor, and the red lights flickered ominously. Stefan stopped before one of the curtains and looked at us.

"Behind this is our Dream Room," he explained. "Every one of these rooms has a theme. The Dream Room is for guests in a light, lush mood. The emphasis is on comfort and shared pleasure." He gripped the curtain and gave us an expectant look. "Would you care to see inside?"

"Show us," Emily urged.

Stefan pulled back the curtain, revealing a room incongruous with the outside settings. It was all blue decor and warm bright light, ethereal and heavenly. A large canopy bed seemed to float in the middle of the room like a giant puffy cumulus cloud. And on the bed, five people writhed together in ecstasy. Three women and two men, all engaging in passioante oral sex with each other in a kind of hedonistic chain.

I looked away at once, ashamed to have caught anyone in the act. But they didn't seem bothered in the least. Most of the participants didn't even notice us. But one of them, a handsome young man, looked up from the pair of thighs he was lodged between and gave us a broad smile before returning to his work.

"Oh, my goodness," Emily exclaimed. She shouldered up to me excitedly. "Look at them!"

It was a wild sight. I'd never seen anyone having sex in front of me before. And now, I was witnessing a five-person daisy chain in that big fluffy bed in a sex club hidden in the basement of an apartment. The nude bodies and cries of ecstasy were a sight. And they got a frustratingly familiar swelling going inside my cage.

"They don't care that anyone's watching?" I piped up, trying to distract myself.

"To them, it's part of the fun," said Stefan.

"Weren't *you* just fucking me in front of a bunch of strangers out at Shining Rock?" Emily asked.

In the whirlwind of our evening, I had completely forgotten about that earlier exhibitionism. "I can't believe that was today."

"And you haven't even cum since that," Emily teased.

Stefan looked impressed. "Sounds like quite a story."

Emily waved him away. "I'm sure you see crazier stuff all the time." She pointed to the action in the bed. "So," she began. "Hypothetically. If we wanted to go over there and join them, how does that work?"

"Usually, those groups form *before* everyone's naked," said Stefan with a grin. "But you can feel free to walk over there and ask to get involved. They're free to say yes or no. And if they say no thanks, they'll say it politely. Once."

"Gotcha," said Emily. Her teeth glittered, and she looked back over at the bed. I almost expected her to walk over and dive in, but she just watched for a few moments. "What other rooms do you have here?"

Stefan gladly led us through the array of other rooms in the club. The variety seemed to cover every possible desire. There was the bondage room, a dark leathery hole decorated with cruel looking implements of iron and leather. Inside, a dominatrix was swatting a crying man strapped into a stockade unmercifully. Emily enjoyed this scene, and told me she wanted to "get one of those outfits". And one of those whips. I shuddered at the thought of what that would mean for me.

We were led to the Water Room, featuring a large communal shower with a few private shower stalls and a couple baths. A group of half a dozen men were engaged in vigorous, sudsy play in the communal shower. Several of them were actually fucking, which shocked me. But Emily was clearly aroused by this man-on-man action, and she squeezed my butt firmly and made lewd comments about my now-lost anal virginity as we watched the group of men continue their rough play.

We saw the glamour room. We saw the blacklight room. The vampire room. The slave room. The schoolhouse. So many different kinky settings established with perfectionist decoration. And each room featured at least a few people enjoying themselves in various degrees of intimacy. As we moved from room to room, my initial shock began to wear off and I was able to be interested in the goings-on in these rooms. Interested, and then turned on watching passionate groups fully enjoying each other in these incredibly detailed settings.

My arousal was heightened by Emily's constant whispering in my ear about how hot the situations were. She was clearly enjoying every minute of our erotic odyssey and encouraging me to do the same. Her hot breath and searching fingers had me straining against my cage, with the plug inside me throbbing. And Stefan was calm and solicitous as he guided us deeper into the club. He did not leer or grope, but instead simply directed us and allowed us to witness the action in each room and react naturally.

Finally, after seeing all of the rooms, we reached the end of the corridor. Stefan opened the simple wooden door at the hallway's end and ushered us inside. Inside was a gorgeous office of shimmering mahogany. The walls were lined with bookcases overflowing with tomes of all sorts. In the center of the office was an ornate wooden desk positioned before an overstuffed chair.

The chair was occupied. A slender girl in a schoolgirl's button-down and skirt lounged back in the chair, her stockinged feet propped up on the desk. Her hair was pulled in pigtails. Everything about her was sexy and sprightly, girlish but in a knowing way. Her head popped up when she heard the door open, and her eyes popped wide with the surprise of a cat being caught with its paw in the fishbowl. "Oh!" she piped up, whipping her legs off the top of the desk at once.

Stefan stopped abruptly and fixed her with an intense stare. "Alexa," he said in a tone whose calm restraint made it all the more threatening. "What are you doing behind daddy's desk, kitten?"

Alexa displayed the book that was propped up by her thighs. "Just reading," she said in a tone of singsong innocence.

Stefan crossed his meaty forearms. "Haven't we talked about this, kitten? You have your own room for your own things. Daddy's office is for daddy. You know the rules."

Emily and I exchanged raised eyebrows. "Kitten?" I mouthed. Emily stifled a giggle. Stefan didn't seem to notice us. He was focused intently on Alexa.

Alexa cocked her shoulders in an insouciant shrug. "I got bored," she said. Then she narrowed her eyes and tightened up her lips in an scowl. "You left me for too long," she pouted.

Stefan took a step forward. "Alexa," he said. "Stand up."

Alexa matched his stare with her insolent scowl. Then, with a slow, defiant movement, she raised her stockinged feet and slid them back onto the desk. The tension in the air was excruciating. Emily and I watched the spectacle with helpless fascination, waiting to see how Stefan would react. Their locked gaze seemed to go on for minutes.

And then Stefan was on her in an instant. I don't know how he managed to get to her so quickly. He did not run. He did not race. He simply strode forward with incredible speed, bearing down on Alexa. Her eyes bugged as Stefan closed in on her, but he was on her before she even managed to pull her feet of the desk.

Alexa squealed as Stefan seized her by the collar. In a flash, he hauled her petite body from the chair with ease, nearly lifting her in the air. Then he shoved her forward, forcing her chest down onto the desk. Papers scattered to the floor as Alexa continued screeching. But Stefan's face was impassive.

Stefan held her there, bent over the desk, pinned down by the force of his powerful hands. Alexa struggled, her feet kicking the air in a futile attempt to free herself of his grip. "That's enough," Stefan growled.

"Let go of me!" Alexa squealed, her feet pumping in the air.

Emily and I exchanged "what-should-we-do-here" looks. Then Stefan addressed us. "Forgive me," he said, his voice calm through the visible strain on his face as he kept Alexa pinned to the desk. He thrust his hips into her butt, pushing her waist into the table hard in a very suggestive pose that also restrained her leg movements. "Alexa is my submissive. And she has a major bratty streak."

"Let me go!" Alexa squealed again. Stefan forced his his hard against her butt. Then he seized her wrists in his hands and forced them down onto the table.

Stefan smiled up at us, a faint sheen of sweat on his face. "She's a handful," he went on. "Probably because she likes to be punished."

"Oh, are you going to *punish* me, Daddy?" Alexa giggled, wiggling her short schoolgirl skirt against his waist.

"You'd like that, wouldn't you, kitten?" Stefan released one of her arms and jerked up her skirt, revealing her pert butt straining against a pair of simple cotton panties. "You naughty little slut," he said. "I should spank this little butt raw to teach you a lesson."

"Oh, yes, daddy," Alexa cooed, closing her eyes.

"You'd like that, wouldn't you?" Stefan raised his burly hand, readying a slap on her butt.

"Oh, yes, daddy," Alexa begged. "Please, spank me."

Stefan held his hand, ready to bring it down hard on Alexa's bottom. Alexa squeezed her eyes shut in anticipation. But the blow never came. Instead, Stefan pulled open one of the desk drawers and pulled out a pair of handcuffs. "I have a better idea," said Stefan. He locked the handcuffs around Alexa's wrists like a cop on his cruiser.

"What are you doing?" Alexa protested. But Stefan wasn't done. He rooted around inside the drawer again and pulled out a leather ball gag with a big red ball.

Alexa's shouting tantrum continued until Stefan slipped the leather strap behind her head and expertly popped the rubber ball inside her mouth. Alexa's shouts were abruptly turned into muffled wails.

Stefan expertly wrapped his strong arm around her waist and hoisted her up over his shoulder. He carried her like that, over his shoulder like a rucksack, while she kicked her legs and struggled to shout through the ballgag. Her slender body seemed to weigh nothing to Stefan, whose calm expression never wavered as he hauled her across the room

He reached an iron pole sunk into the ground near the far wall. The pole, running up to the ceiling, was fitted with a series of loops and hooks on its way up that seemed able to accomodate the most devious devices imaginable. Stefan gently slung Alexa from his shoulder and set her down on the ground. He ignored her continued cries and circled around her, taking out a leather strap. With a few deft movements, he looped the strap through her handcuffs and lashed it to the pole, leaving Alexa seated on the ground, hands cuffed behind her, tied up to the iron pole. She tried to scream, but the ball gag allowed only the slightest sound.

When he was finished, Stefan stepped back to admire his handiwork. Then he fixed Alexa with a devious look. "Stay here, kitten," he said. He reached down and tenderly stroked her cheek "Don't worry. Your punishment is only starting."

Then he wheeled and marched back to his desk. "Come," he beckoned, directing us to a pair of guest chairs opposite the overstuffed one behind the desk.

We took our seats and waited as Stefan rummaged through a cabinet by the wall. He returned to the desk with a glass bottle filled with brown liquor and three ornate tumblers. "Again, I apologize," he said, his eyes darting over to Alexa. She glowered at us from her bondage on the floor across the room, seething with indignation at her plight. Stefan smiled at us. "Like I said, she's a little brat. She loves saying no, because she likes to get punished. I can't just spank her when she's bad, because that's exactly what she wants."

"So, this is all part of your game?" Emily asked.

"Of course," said Stefan, pouring drinks into our glasses. "We have our rules, and we have our limitations. All decided when she first agreed to serve me."

Alexa made some angry noises. She was a pathetic creature there on the floor, her schoolgirl skirt flounced up over her thighs, her eyes wide and teary. "She likes being treated like that?" I asked.

"She loves it," Stefan told me. "There's a joy in eroticism far beyond the simple pleasures of the flesh. Our deepest happiness comes from finding someone who understands our desires. Someone we can be our authentic selves around." He gestured to Alexa. "Alexa likes playing the brat. She craves attention, and gets it by acting out. She likes to push buttons. But deep down, she just wants to know that someone cares about her."

"So why are you ignoring her, then?"

Stefan smiled. "It's all part of the game," he answered. "All she wants is my attention. Denying her what she wants only increases her desire for it. I'm going to leave her there until she's dying for me. And then I'll have my way with her." Alexa made a muffled, desperate moan from the floor.

Stefan ignored her and pushed a glass toward me. "So," he said, looking between me and Emily. "Tell me about yourselves. What is the nature of your relationship?"

"Well…" I began halfheartedly.

"We're pretty new to all this," Emily admitted, taking her drink. We followed Stefan's lead and sipped what turned out to be some fine scotch. "But I'd say I'm definitely the one in charge of us."

Stefan raised his eyebrows. "A dominant woman," he said. "I like it." He turned to me. "So, that makes you the submissive, then?"

"I don't…" I stammered. "I mean, I'm not sure. This is all so new to me."

"Does she tell you what to do?" Stefan probed.

"Does she like to tease you?"

"We just started, really," Emily admitted.

"That's fine." Stefan took another drink. There was a playful glimmer in his eye. "So, what have you been trying out?"

Emily and I looked to each other briefly. The memories of the past day and a half ran through our minds simultaneously before we both blushed and looked away. "Well," Emily began. "It all started with me telling him some dirty stories about my past."

Stefan stroked his chin. "Interesting." He addressed me. "And you enjoyed hearing these stories about her past?"

My face was flushed beet red. "Well, I-" I stammered, trying to find the least humiliating response.

Stefan just smiled. "It's ok," he said. "These things can be hard to talk about sometimes. There's a lot of issues of masculinity wrapped up in your feelings about your partner enjoying herself with other men. But that's probably exactly why you find that image so powerfully erotic."

"Yeah," I agreed. I found myself responding candidly, more candidly than I imagined I could talk about my strange fantasies with a stranger. But the way he addressed me, so thoughtful and genuinely interested, made me feel like I was the only person in the room. It felt safe to open up. "It's so odd. She was telling me all these things about the… stuff she used to do. And it made me feel frustrated and jealous, but at the same time, I got…"

"Turned on?" Stefan offered.

"Yeah," I admitted. My cock twitched through its cage. "Really turned on."

Stefan spread his hands. "Well, that's all that matters," he said. "The fact that you had a response to it. There's no need to feel guilty or ashamed about reacting the way you did." He smiled over to Emily. "You have a beautiful, sexy girlfriend," he said, and Emily blushed. We heard noises of protest from Alexa through her ball gag.

"And I'm sure you must feel jealous and protective of her. And most guys have conflicted feelings about their girlfriends' past. You want to be the only one for them. I've struggled with that too," he admitted. "Very badly in the past. But I've found that sublimating that jealously into erotic energy is the best way of handling that kind of feeling."

He turned to Emily. "And how do you feel about sharing all those details of your past?"

Emily gave a happy smile. "It's really nice," she said. "I was so worried I wouldn't be able to find a boyfriend who accepted my past. Turning it into this fun, sexy game has been such a huge relief." Her hand found mine, and our fingers intertwined by our chairs. She flashed me a warm look.   'It gets me really turned on, too."

Stefan gave an approving nod. "That's great." He leaned back in his chair. "So, what other fun things have you been getting up to in this exploration period?"

Once again, I couldn't hold Stefan's gaze. "I-"

"I've been teasing him," Emily said. She gave my hand a reassuring squeeze. "Getting him really turned on but denying him. Keeping him frustrated and on the edge. It's so hot."

"Oh, that's wonderful," Stefan said. "Taking control over your partner's orgasm can be such a powerful feeling." He looked over to me. "And giving up control can work the same way. I've experienced both before. Allowing your partner to take control of your pleasure can make that pleasure so much better."

I remembered the intensity of my orgasm the night before, teased out of me by Emily's lightest touch. And I sensed the volcanic warmth inside me and knew my next would be even more powerful. "It is."

"Actually…" said Emily. She looked shy, but she had a wicked twinkle in her eye. "We got something to help with that." She held up the key to the cage like a trophy. The hot feeling flooded my face again.

A broad grin broke over Stefan's rugged face. "I'm

guessing you just purchased that from Nancy?"

"You guessed it," Emily grinned.

"No wonder she sent you to me," Stefan mused. "She must have sensed you were an adventurous couple. Stepping into chastity after just a couple days of teasing is a big step." He fixed me with a look that was was warm but powerful. "How does it feel?"

I tried to hold his gaze. "It's strange," I said. "I've been so frustrated all day. And now this makes it so much worse."

"But are you enjoying it?"

I thought about the frustrated tension locked inside me. The feeling of being teased and denied by Emily all day, multiplied tenfold now by my plastic prison. How could I enjoy such degredation? And yet... her control over the key was so tantalizing. The knowledge of the powerful sweet release right at her fingertips drove me wild. If it was anything like the release from last night- and I expected it would be even better- than this whole experience would be worth it. "I am," I admitted.

Stefan leaned forward on the desk. His hypnotic eyes held me in their power like a snake. "Show me."

He did not glare or shout or insist. He simply told me. And his words were all the more powerful for it. I couldn't sense Alexa or even Emily though she squeezed my hand. I was simply guided by the overwhelming power of his gaze as I rose obediently to my feet.

I was unbuckling my pants when I remembered that they contained more secrets than just my chastity. I hesitated. But at that point it was too late. And slowly I unzipped the jeans, revealing a flash of the soft pink lace-fringe panties Emily had given me. Stefan's eyes dilated as he watched, but he did not speak or more. He simply watched as I slid. my jeans down, past my waist, revealing everything.

Suddenly I felt all three sets of eyes in the room fixate. "Well, now," Stefan breathed, shifting in his seat. Even Alexa tried to squeal from the ground. Stefan's eyes traveled down to the panties without hurry.

Embarrassed and ready to get the ordeal over with, I pulled the panties aside. My cage-bound cock flopped out. It felt so small constricted in its plastic sheath. But that wasn't my fault- it was the sheath's. Something about that was strangely reassuring. I stood still, blushing furiously, with the cage cupped in my hand to display it.

"Very nice," said Stefan. "Locked like a good submissive should be." His eyes glittered with mirth. "You like wearing panties?"

My blush answered for me. "Those are mine," Emily laughed, hiding her face in her hands. "I was going to wear them tonight."

Stefan smiled at her. "I see," he said. "I'm sure they look fantastic on you." His lip twitched again. "So, if those are yours, then what are *you* wearing tonight?"

Emily looked over to me briefly for reassurance and flashed a little smile. Still blushing, I thought about the secret under her dress and smiled back. She took this as a signal. Slowly, she parted her legs in the chair. Then she pulled up the hemline of her dress, revealing her smooth thighs all the way up until she reached her waist. With a little smile, she flicked up the rest of the skirt, revealing her smooth cunt naked between her legs.

I couldn't believe my girlfriend was showing off her naked pussy to a complete stranger. I should have been furious. I should have punched him in the nose and dragged Emily out of there right away. But standing there in those girly panties, holding my locked-up cock, there was no way I could protest. I felt the same way about her lewd display as I did about how tiny my cock looked in its cage- the loss of control made it all easier. I could just give up and let it happen.

Alexa was practically screaming with rage through her ball gag as she watched Stefan ogle Emily's bare pussy. But I sensed in her cries that same sense of safety in the lack of control. Her tears and screams were like my silence: our shameful cope with something beyond our control that somehow made it all easier to bear.

Stefan looked between both of us, sizing up the situation. "So, what do we have here? A boy in panties and a chastity cage, locked up and in control of his girlfriend. His sexy girlfriend who teases him with stories about her slutty past. And who is currently showing her bare pussy off to a stranger."

"He's wearing a butt plug too!" Emily smirked.

"I should have guessed," Stefan chuckled. "Well, you're really quite a kinky pair. I think we could have a lot of fun together, if you'd like."

At this point there was no doubt we would go along with Stefan's plans. The thrill of Alexa watching bound and helpless from the floor only added to our eagerness. Emily and I shared a quick glance and *why-not* shrug. We were both ready to see where the night took us.

Stefan rose from his desk again, reminding us of his powerful, intimidating physique. He pushed his rolled-up dress sleeves to his elbows and fixed me with a look. "Finish taking off those pants," he said.

I kicked my shoes off obediently and pulled my pants to the floor. As I did, Stefan circled around the table.

"Sit," he ordered, and I dropped back to my seat. He spoke in simple commands, like he was training dogs. And this somehow made him all the easier to obey.

Stefan motioned for me to put my hands on the armrests. As soon as I did, he fastened my wrists to the chair's arms with a pair of heavy leather straps. They were cool against my arms, and he tightened them up until they bound me firmly to the chair. I tried to struggle- no good. I could barely move an inch.

Stefan circled back around the chair. The hairs on the back of my neck stood as I felt his presence behind me. Then he seized the chair by its arms and scooted it around in a circle, whirling me toward the center of the room. From this point, I could see the door we'd come though, and Alexa chained up and seething by the floor. And at the center of it all stood Stefan, fully in control.

He crooked a finger at Emily. "Come." She obeyed at once, trotting right over to him. Stefan stopped her just a few inches from him with an outstretched hand. Then he looked down at me with a playful smile.

"Look at you," he said. "Hands tied. Cock tied up. All locked up and helpless in your girly panties. And you know what I'm about to do?" His hand traveled to the zipper of his leather pants. There was a wicked glint in his eye. "I'm about to make your girlfriend suck my dick."

Emily's eyes widened at this, and she shot me a quick look to see how I would react. I struggled against my bonds in the chair to no avail. The only result of my thrashing was to force myself against the hard chair seat, working the plug deeper into me. But I did not speak up, although I could have. I simply watched, helplessly fascinated, waiting to see what would happen. Alexa would have screamed if she could, but all her words were choked out by the ball gag restricting her mouth. She seethed with fury on the floor, kicking her stockinged legs out in a whirlwind.

Stefan ignored Alexa's tantrum. He fixed Emily with that powerful, irresistible stare. "Get on your knees." She obeyed, slowly, sinking down to her knees while holding Stefan's gaze. I saw her and Stefan in profile, facing toward each other, holding eye contact, Emily on the ground, Stefan looming over her. He unbuckled his belt and slowly worked his zipper down.

I struggled more against my bonds but there was nothing I could do. Despite the churning in my gut, my cock twinged with a strange anticipation. Stefan reached into his leather pants with a smirk. And then he pulled it out. His cock. A thick, veiny tube, swollen with blood but only half-hard. Even Emily seemed taken aback by its powerful girth. He let it dangle down, swaying like a threatening pendulum.

"Take it," Stefan ordered. I watched helplessly as Emily reached with a tentative hand. She moved on his cock like it was a wild creature that she was afraid would bite her. She didn't look at me; her eyes were fixed on the thick cock dangling before her face. Stefan just watched, eyes trained on her. Her fingers closed around the shaft.

"Wow," Emily breathed. "It's so thick." She worked the cock gently with her hand, stroking it gently up and down. It was huge in her delicate fingers, even as it hung half-hard. *Oh god,* I thought, feeling the strange twitching inside my cage. *She's touching another guy's cock right in front of me.*

"Kiss it," Stefan ordered. Emily dutifully lifted the cock to her face. I thought I saw her eyes flicker over to me for an instant. But then she looked up at Stefan with reverent eyes. And she lifted his heavy cock and brought it to her lips. She kissed it softly on the tip, gently at first. I squirmed in my chair, inadvertently driving the butt plug deeper inside me. To my shame, my cock was swelling in its restrictive cage at the sight of my gorgeous girlfriend on her knees, holding this thick cock to her lips.

She planted kisses down the shaft while keeping her adoring, loving eyes fixed on Stefan's. The wet sound of her lips on his cock filled the room. Stefan reached down to stroke Emily's hair as she moved her mouth across his cock. "Good girl," he breathed. His fingers tightened in her hair. "Now lick it. Get it nice and wet."

Emily let her tongue drop from her mouth. Stefan groaned as Emily licked his cock up and down, slicking up his thickening shaft with her spit. She ran her lips and tongue up and down his ever-growing member until it glistened. My cock pulsated inside its cage. The view was pure torture to me.

"Now suck," Stefan commanded. He pulled Emily back by her hair until the cock was pointed at her face like a weapon. I squirmed in my seat in disbelief of what I was about to witness. Her lips parted, and slowly she slid her head forward, taking his cock inside her mouth. She took him down inch my inch, slowly but relentlessly moving forward. I was in shock at how much of his cock had disappeared down her throat on that first push. She kept moving forward, taking him deeper, until I could see him bulging in the back of her throat. When she had swallowed him down all the way to the base of his shaft, she held him still there, her watery eyes staring up at him with a look of utter devotion.

"That's a good girl," Stefan groaned. "Look at you, taking the entire thing in your mouth all at once. You've got some practice with a cock, don't you?"

Emily tried to answer, but her voice was as muffled as Alexa's. She gave a simple nod and a choking affirmative. Stefan smiled at this. "Good girl," he repeated, stroking her hair. "What a good little slut."

He held her head still, his cock pushing in the back of her throat, and looked over at me. "Look at that," he said. "Your girlfriend has my cock shoved all the way down her throat. Did you see how easily she took it all? What a little whore you ended up with." I swallowed hard, struggling in my leather straps, but said nothing. Stefan smirked at me. "Don't pretend you don't like it," he went on. "I bet your little cock is straining in your cage so much right now. Isn't it?" He was right; my dick was fully constricted by the cage as it tried to swell up from the sight of Emily deepthroating Stefan's massive cock. My cheeks burned with shame, but I couldn't look away.

"That's right," Stefan said. "I'm going to show you how your girlfriend treats a real man." He allowed Emily to slip her head back, and she choked slightly as his cock slid free of her throat. "Good girl," he said, twisting her hair up in his fingers. "Keep going."

Stefan used her hair to guide her head back and forth, working his cock in and out of Emily's mouth. The room was filled with the sound of her mouth and throat feasting on his meat, and the plaintive choking wails of Alexa tied up on the floor nearby. She and I watched on in frustrated helplessness as Alexa serviced Stefan from her knees. She worked him expertly, using that magical touch I had felt from her before and craved so desperately. She would lick him up and down, massaging his balls with her lips and stroking his shaft before taking the whole thing back in her mouth and swallowing him deep. And all the while Stefan praised her for being a good girl, and teased me and Alexa with his cruel, enticing words.

"Such a good little slut," he murmured. He looked pointedly at Alexa as he pumped his cock in and out of Emily's throat hard. "You see that?" he teased, watching Alexa's eyes bug out as she struggled with her bonds. "When you're a bad girl, you don't get to enjoy daddy's treats. Someone else gets to." Alexa whined helplessly from the ground, her hands thrashing against her cuffs. "Bad little kitten," Stefan scolded her. "Breaking all the rules. I'm going to make you pay for being such a disobedient little brat."

"And you," he said, turning to me. "Sad little sissy boy. Watching your girlfriend suck my cock. Can't you see how much she loves it?" He suddenly pulled his cock from Emily's mouth and jerked her head back by the hair.

Then he leaned forward and kissed her deeply, their wet tongues working together as she continued stroking his cock. Then he pulled away abruptly and seized his cock in his hand. He began roughly smacking his hard dick against Emily's lips and cheek, filling the air with the wet smack of his cock on her face. "Tell him you love it," he growled.

"I love it," Emily moaned through the cock slapping against her face. "I love your cock."

Stefan jerked her head forward and forced his cock through her lips again. He pumped it deep, hips moving forward like pistons. Tears streamed down Emily's cheeks as Stefan fucked her face, bulging her throat with the imprint of his cock. Then he pulled himself free again, leaving wet trails of saliva dangling from his cock. "Tell him you're a dirty little slut," he ordered, slapping her face with his dick again.

"I am," Emily panted. "I'm a dirty little slut," she said between the heavy slaps of Stefan's cock on her hungry tongue. "I'm a little whore. A dirty cock hungry whore."

"That's good," Stefan said. He pumped her throat with his cock again, fucking her mouth hard and fast. then pulled out and jerked her head to face at me, while he continued working his cock with his fist close to Emily's face. "Tell him you're sorry."

"I'm so sorry, baby," she panted through mouthfuls of cock. She locked eyes with me, her face flushed and red, her eyeliner running in tears down her cheeks, lipstick smeared, hair disheveled. "I'm just a filthy, cheating whore. I try to be good, but I just can't keep my legs closed." The sight drove me wild. My cock spasmed helplessly in its cage, filling me with an overwhelming insane frustration.

"Why not?" Stefan asked, working his cock deep in her throat again.

"Because I'm a slut," she gasped as he pulled himself free. "A cock-craving dirty little tramp."

"You love being treated like a little whore?" Stefan said, slapping her with his cock again.

"I love it," she moaned. "I need it. I deserve it."

"You want my cum?" Stefan growled, jerking her head back. He stroked his cock furiously, working himself to the edge. A sheen of sweat appeared on his forehead and his breathing tightened.

"Oh, yes, please," Emily begged. She opened her mouth and let her tongue fall open, shamelessly yearning for his load. Her knees were splayed out, the dress tangled between her thighs. It was the sexiest sight I'd ever witnessed. "Please, give me your cum.'

Stefan held her back and continued stroking his rock-hard cock as Emily made little moans. He looked at me, and then at Alexa. "Watch this, now," he ordered us. "Watch this little slut take my load."

And then in an instant, he had reached the point of no return. "Oh, god," he grunted. "Take my load, whore." And then his cock exploded. The first rope splattered across her lips and cheek, dripping all the way into her hair. He jerked her head forward and shoved his cock between her lips, where he continued spraying his load until it was dribbling from the corners of her lips. He pulled out again, spraying her face with another hot rope of his cum, before slipping his cock between her lips again and finishing the job.

When he was finished, he pulled his softening cock free and gave a grunting sigh of satisfaction. "Fuck, that was so hot," he panted. He looked down at Emily's cum-streaked face and patted her cheek gently. "Don't swallow," he ordered. "Hold it all there."

Emily closed her mouth obediently, holding his load between her lips. Stefan seized her under the arms and hauled her to her feet. "Come," he ordered, beckoning her to me. He smirked over at me. "Did your girlfriend do a good job?" he asked.

My cock was spasming relentlessly in its cage, and the pressure of the plug inside me had caused me to leak a dribble of cum through the cage. My cheeks burned; I couldn't take my eyes off Emily, bedraggled and flushed, her face streaked with cum, her mouth closed around the load she held inside. "Answer me," Stefan snapped sharply.

"Yes," I murmured helplessly.

"Yes, what?"

"Yes, she did a good job sucking your cock."

"Yes, she did," Stefan murmured. He looked between me and Emily. "And you should tell her she did a good job. How about a kiss?"

My stomach did a somersault at the thought of kissing her cum-stained lips. But I could not resist as Emily advanced on me, her eyes burning and hypnotic. I could smell him on her as she neared me, a hot, musty odor that bewitched both of us. The sight of her had me completely mesmerized. I couldn't think straight. My thoughts swam. And suddenly, she was bending over to me in my captivity in the chair. Her mouth met mine. Her lips parted. And we kissed.

She kissed me deeply, her tongue invading my mouth. How I had longed to feel her sweet kiss again as I watched her. But as she opened her mouth to meet mine, Stefan's hot load flooded into mine, filling my mouth. Emily worked her tongue against mine as we shared his load. It was thick and sticky but nowhere near as vile as I'd feared. But the humiliation of this hot and slippery makeout session, and my enjoyment of it, was almost too much for me to bear. Yet still my cock struggled in its cage, and the burning desire inside me only intensified.

"Swallow it down," Stefan ordered, and I obeyed unthinkingly. When I was done eating his cum from Emily's mouth, he directed me to clean up the rest. "Lick it up," Stefan urged. "Eat every drop, you pathetic little worm." Using my tongue, I licked the streams of cum that splattered across her face, drawing his sticky load from her cheeks and lips and taking it into my mouth.

Emily practically purred with pleasure at the sensation of my tongue on her skin, and her fingers sweetly traced my neck and cheek as I cleaned her up. She wiped a dribbling strand from the corner of my lip and pushed it into my mouth with her finger. "Good boy," she whispered, watching me suck the cum from her finger. "Good, sweet boy."

"That was amazing," Stefan breathed, zipping up his pants again. "I think I'm going to like playing with you two." He directed Emily away from me and then approached and stood before me. His dark eyes were probing but somehow kind, like he was a benevolent god. "How do you feel?"

I tried to keep his eyes, even though I could still taste him on my lips. I'd never done anything so humiliating in my life. My cock was throbbing through its cage. I was so hungry, desperate, yearning, frustrated, overwhelmed... driven nearly mad by the range of emotions that bombarded me. Stefan leaned closer to me. His eyes held me captive. His voice was a low insistent growl. "Now it's your turn."

I sat frozen as he unbuckled the leather straps binding my wrists to the chair arms. He tossed aside the straps and beckoned me to my feet. I followed him in a trance, not speaking, barely even thinking. The hot yearning inside me had swollen to the point where it was melting my brain into the simple madness of desire. I could barely even consider what was happening anymore.

Stefan led me to a wood-and-leather pommel horse stationed near the wall. On first glance it looked like just part of the furnishing of his sophisticated office, but as I approached I wondered- *what the hell is this thing doing in an office?* I got my answer soon, when Stefan smacked the leather butt of the horse. "Hands up," he said. I mechanically obeyed, sliding my hands up onto the soft leather of the pommel horse. Stefan took my wrists from the other side of the leather horse. I caught just the shadow of a glimmer in his eye before he gave me a sudden yank forward, pulling me across the horse. My surprised shout was suffocated out by my stomach smashing into the leather horse.

As I lay bent over the leather horse, trying to get my bearings, Stefan went to work with detached mastery. He secured my wrists to a pair of metal handholds with the leather straps, restricting me to my bent-over position. My cheeks burned at this humiliating exposure of my panty-clad butt, which stuck out behind me like I was engaged in a depraved mating ritual. I tried to wiggle myself to some degree of modesty, but there was no escape.

"Look at that little sissy boy," Stefan laughed, fixing Emily with his eyes. "His butt stuck up in the air. He looks like a bigger whore than you like that." He gestured to me with his head. "Go over to him."

Emily walked over to me. I felt her presence nearing, and my cock squirmed inside its cage. As she approached, Stefan walked back over to the desk while continuing to give orders. "Unbutton his shirt," he said. I felt Emily's hands slide around my body to my back. She pressed against me from behind, pushing her hips into my butt as she reached up to my throat to take my top button. I couldn't move for the bonds strapping me to the horse. I just relaxed into the feeling of her press against me, removing my buttons one by one. Her hips pressed the plug deeper into my butt, causing my cock to tremble inside its cage.

I heard Stefan rooting around in the desk drawers as Emily unbuttoned my shirt. When she finished, he ordered her to strip down my panties. She obeyed, pulling the soft pink lace down to my heels and exposing my chastity cage and butt plug.

"Look at that little whore," Stefan cackled. "Locked up with a plug in his ass. And what an ass it is," he said. "It looks just like a girl's. I bet he'd love to have a real cock shoved up there, huh?"

"No-" I protested weakly, but Stefan cut me off.

"Silence!" he commanded. "If he can't be a good boy and be quiet, we better make him be quiet. Pick up those panties and shove them in his mouth."

Emily followed these instructions, wadding up her soft cotton panties into a ball and forcing them against my face. I resisted, only just, before allowing her to fill my mouth with the soft fabric I'd leaked cum all over from my cage. When I was properly gagged, Stefan approached again from behind. I couldn't see what he carried with him, but I suspected it was going to be trouble for me.

"Listen up," he said to Emily. "I'm going to teach you how to break in your little subby slave boy. The secret is to show no mercy. Remember, he's a depraved little pervert who loves being punished."

I found myself locking eyes with Alexa from her spot on the floor. I couldn't read the expression on her face. Contempt? Jealousy? Emily and Stefan were hidden behind me. My spine tingled at the thought of what they might do to me. "Grab his chastity," Stefan ordered.

I felt Emily's delicate hand close around the cage, holding my caged cock and balls in a firm hand. My cock twitched inside the cage, desperate for freedom. "See that?" Stefan said. "Can you feel how badly he wants out?"

"It's so full," Emily breathed. "Your balls are so heavy."

I tried to speak, but the panties suffocated the words. Emily gave a firm tug on my cock and balls, making me squeak with surprise. Stefan cackled as he watched Emily tug me more, stretching my skin and causing my eyes to fill up. The feeling was pain, pleasure, and bitter frustration all wrapped up in an overwhelming feeling inside me. And as she tugged on the cage, she began pushing on the base of the plug inside me, working it deep against my prostate.

"Take this," I heard Stefan say from behind. I didn't know what he was referring to, but I felt a twinge of fear inside me. Emily suddenly released my chastity and buttplug and stepped back. Despite my embarrassment, the sensation of her massage had felt so good and she had stopped so abruptly that my body was begging for more. Involuntarily I stuck my ass out, wiggling it shamelessly like an animal in heat, begging for her to continue pressing on the plug. "Aw, look at your little sub boy. He's in heat," Stefan laughed. "Why don't you give him a taste of that little toy?"

I half expected a pleasurable feeling, but instead I was startled by a sudden *slap* of a flogger on my ass. I yelped in pain and tried to jerk to my feet, but the leather straps held me tight to the pony. My cries were muffled out by the panties stuffed in my mouth. A second later, another sharp blow smacked into my bare butt, nearly blinding me with the pain.

"That's good," Stefan encouraged Emily. "Good, now rub his little cock again." She seized my cage in her hand, her fingers stroking the base of my balls. She used the flogger to press the butt plug deeper into me as she tugged on my chastity, torturing me with the sweet unreachable pleasure I craved so badly. And then she reared back and landed another stinging blow on my butt.

This punishment continued, alternating sweet teasing rubbing and hard whipping, until I was nearly out of my mind. Tears streamed down my cheeks as I was reduced to a shuddering mess by all the feelings welling up in me. I locked eyes with Alexa, who was similarly tortured by being ignored, worked into a frenzy by watching me be soothed and punished over and over by Emily under Stefan's guidance.

Stefan gave her different implements to use on me, each having a different but still keenly painful effect on me. She used a riding crop to land a series of smart slaps to the base of my balls, causing me to rise up on my toes in agony. She whipped me in long, powerful strokes with a leather belt, raising welts across my butt and back. She raked a metal claw down the flesh of my thighs. And between all of this torture, she teased my cage and plug. This sweet denial became a torture worse than the pain, driving me wild with my desire for the completion that was denied to me.

Finally, Stefan instructed Emily to pull the buttplug free from my yearning ass. She did, slowly drawing it out by the base. I felt like my stomach was turning inside out as the plug stretched me open again, holding against my tight hole before I opened up and allowed it to slip free. The sudden emptiness was startling. But it did not last long.

I lay across the leather horse, my chastity cage dangling down, my ass raised up into the air, panting for breath. Behind, I heard Emily fumbling with some new devilry given by Stefan. I shuddered to think what would happen to me next, and yet I somehow yearned for it. "That looks great on you," Stefan said. *What does?*

I got my answer a moment later. There was the pop of a lid. A wet smear. And then a slick dribble down the center of my hole that made me shiver. Lube. *What could-* and suddenly her hands were on me. One firmly gripping my hip, holding me still. The other guiding a thick silicone rod up against my ass. *Oh god. It's a strap-on.*

"You like my cock?" Emily asked, teasing the silicone dildo down my hole to my taint. "It's a lot bigger than yours," she said, pushing it against the base of my balls and rubbing it on my chastity cage. "You still want to fuck me in the ass?"

I gave a muffled moan of affirmative through the panties constricting my mouth. "Well," Emily laughed, smacking the dong against my hole. "It's only fair that you know what it feels like for me."

And with that, she pushed the head of her silicone cock into me. I gasped as my flesh parted to take her in. It seemed to catch on my entrance, sticking and squeezing and forcing me open in an unbearable tearing pain. I thought I would surely have to stop her before she ripped me in half. But then my hole stretched open to take her. A long, sweetly agonizing stretching filling of my ass as the silicone cock slid deep into me, wrenching me open inch by inch. Every limb of my body trembled from the almighty opening inside me. And then the cockhead pressed against that hard nut of pleasure deep inside me. This nearly drove me out of my mind. My knees buckled, but Emily held me firmly by the hips, her fingers pinching into me.

"Good boy," she breathed, resting her body up against me. She allowed me a short reprieve to get used to the stretching inside me. The thing felt as big as her entire forearm. All I could do was shudder weakly as she tenderly stroked my hair. "Good boy," she whispered, caressing me. "You took it all."

Then she began to pull it out. I thought all my organs would come with it. An overwhelming, intense suction of my guts, pulling through my stretched-out hole. I gasped, and the panties stuffed in my mouth tumbled out onto the floor. I hardly noticed this. All I could focus on was the incredible sensation of the strapon slipping back out of me. Emily held it steady just as it reached the tip, teasing my entrance just as it gripped her. And then she worked it back inside me, another long slow thrust that took the wind out of me. The pressure inside my balls from all the days' frustration was so keenly focused that when the cock pressed against my prostate, I almost came. My cock spasmed wildly, stretching to fill the cage around me.

"That's good," said Stefan. He was close behind me, watching Emily drive the strapon into me. "Keep going. Fuck him harder."

Emily picked up the pace. She began to drive the strapon deep into me in long, steady thrusts. Each one felt like a fist driving into my stomach, sending waves through my entire body. Yet the steady hammering pressure on my prostate was an overwhelming pleasure, filling me with a hot exquisite pressure that made me feel on the verge of orgasm the entire time. And so I eased into Emily's firm grip on my hips and surrendered, arching out my back and offering myself up to her as she pounded me deeper and harder, each thrust forcing a ragged cry from my mouth.

"Listen to that little slut moan," Stefan said mockingly.

Emily giggled and started fucking me harder. "Yes, you are," she moaned, slamming her hips against me. "You are a dirty little slut with this cock in your ass." She reared back and landed a hard slap on my already-bruised ass, making me yelp. "Look at you, you dirty whore. Moaning like a girl while getting your ass fucked."

The constant stream of pressure and pleasure pulsating through my body made me unable to respond. I just lay back, sinking deeper into the feeling as Emily ravaged me. She fucked me hard and deep, slapping my ass over and over while she pounded me senseless. And all the while she whispered a constant stream of degradation to me, calling me a slut and a whore and making me beg for her to fuck me harder. And I shamelessly complied, lost in the desperate feeling inside me and feeling constantly just on the edge of a release that never came.

Finally, Emily sank into me, exhausted. I felt the beads of sweat dripping from her has she caught her breath against me. "Oh, fuck," she gasped. "This is so hot." I could only moan weakly and burrow my ass into her hips, desperate for the pounding to continue.

"Look at him!" Stefan cackled. "The little slut still wants more!"

"I need a break," Emily laughed. "This fucking is

harder than it looks. I've got to give it to you guys."

She started to pull out, but Stefan stopped her. "Stay," he ordered. She held herself deep inside me, keeping a steady pressure inside me. Her hands slid up my damp unbuttoned shirt, fingernails tracing my sweaty back.

Stefan moved closer. "Look at you," he said. "Such a sexy little minx in that dress. Getting yourself all worked up fucking your boyfriend. I think it's your turn for a nice hard fucking."

I heard him unbuckling his pants behind us. Then suddenly he shoved her forward, pushing her into me. Emily's weight fell against me until she was practically laying across me like a table. This forced the strapon deeper into me as she angled her perfect butt to offer it up. We both breathed together. I felt Stefan jerk up her dress, flipping it over her back. And then Emily gasped as he slid his thick cock deep into her cunt from behind.

Emily gripped me tight, her hands wrapping around my chest, her full body leaned against my back as

Stefan drove himself deep into her. I could feel the heat of his body on top of her, the vibrations of his thrusts against her. "Oh, fuck," she moaned, her breath hot in my ear. "His cock feels so good inside me."

"You like that, slut?" Stefan growled. The air was filled with the hard slaps of his thighs against her butt as he fucked her hard and deep. My entire body shook from the weight of Emily being pounded as she lay across my back. I felt him jerk Emily's head back by her hair, forcing a desperate cry from her. "Tell your little boyfriend how much you love my cock."

"I love it," she gasped. "Oh, fuck, it feels amazing."

"Grab his chastity," he ordered, Emily's fingers snaked around my waist and seized my cock and balls. Every thrust of Stefan's cock inside her forced the strapon deep into my ass and made her tug my chastity hard. I was practically weeping with the desperate yearning for release, and the humiliation of this man fucking my girlfriend on top of me. She moaned like a whore as he pounded her without mercy, driving his cock into her fast and deep as she begged for more.

By the time he reached his full speed I was practically a pile of goo on the ground. My cock leaked steadily from the pressure inside me, and my eyes rolled back in my head. The heat of Emily's dripping body against me and the shameful thrill of her lustful moans in my ear was too much to bear, and yet I still could not cum. I just moaned, savoring the incredible thrill of the moment and the desperation and the hunger.

"Oh, god," Emily cried in a ragged voice. "Oh, god, I'm going to cum." She nearly collapsed on me as an earthquake of an orgasm rocked through her body. She sobbed helplessly, legs shaking, hands squeezing tight, screaming out in pure pleasure as the sensation washed over her.

Stefan increased his speed, hammering her brutally as the orgasm washed through her body. "That's right, slut," he barked, and I felt his hand close around her throat. "I'm about to fill up your cunt, you whore." He continued slamming against her, deep and hard as he worked himself closer and closer. "Oh, fuck," he growled.

"I'm about to cum."

"Cum inside me," Emily begged in her half-wild voice. "Please, fill me up!"

"Take it, slut," Stefan cried, burying himself deep in her. He gave an almighty groan as he forced himself through her, and Emily moaned long and loud as she felt his hot load fill her up. She lay across my back, panting hard, her hands wrapped around me, as Stefan pulsed inside her.

"Oh, fuck, that was good," Stefan grunted. He slipped out of her, and I felt his load dribbling down onto my thighs from Emily's ravaged cunt.

When Emily caught her breath, she gripped me firmly by my raw, welted ass. Squeezing for leverage, she slowly began to slip the strapon out of me. It was a new agony, feeling her silicone cock slip free of my ravaged hole. But she was gentle and took her time pulling it free from me. I gave a final gasp as it slipped out, and felt suddenly barren and empty without its pressure inside me.

"I think he's missing something," Stefan laughed. I heard him hand something to Emily. And then there was a familiar pressure against my exposed hole.

"Shhh…" Emily soothed, working the butt plug back inside my ravaged ass. She stroked me gently on the back as she pressed the plug in deep, until it was nestled against the tender nut of pleasure at the back. My cock twitched again, leaking another stream of fluid.

As Emily replaced the buttplug, Stefan moved around the pommel horse to undo my straps. "Nice work," he said, releasing my wrists. I wrung out my hands hard, pins and needles from the rush of blood tickling up through my fingers.

I hauled myself to my feet, my knees weak, barely able to move. The first thing I did was look for Emily. She was an incredible sight, shining with a wild beauty that stopped my heart. Her hair was tangled, her cheeks were flushed red, her dress disheveled. Around her waist she still wore the strapon, a large purple dildo glistening with lube that attached to her waist with a belt. Her stockings were torn. Her lipstick was smeared. She was gorgeous.

I flew to her in rush, and our mouths met in a passionate kiss. We drank in each others' love, savoring the feeling of our reunion together. We were both flushed and weak and giddy in our arousal, arms wrapped around each other, squeezing and caressing sweetly.

"I see you enjoyed yourselves," Stefan laughed, watching us from the side. We turned to him, giggling with embarrassment at how caught up in the moment we had been with each other.

"That was incredible," Emily breathed, squeezing my hand.

"I'm glad," Stefan told her, his eyes twinkling. He looked at me. "What did you think?"

Still flushed from my strange mixture of shame and pleasure and frustrated denial, I could barely muster a response. I took a minute to compose myself under Stefan's watchful gaze. Then I met his eyes. "I loved it," I admitted.

"Well, good," Stefan chuckled. He glanced down at my chastity cage. "You must still be pretty frustrated, though."

My cock throbbed in its cage. "Yes," I admitted, looking down.

Stefan laughed again. "Well, you've been a great sport here. I think you've earned a little reward. And I think I've got an idea of how we can do that."

He walked over to Alexa, who glowered at him from her cuffed position on the floor. "Ok, kitten," he said, talking to her in a soothing steady voice like he was approaching a wild dog. "Now, be a good girl for me here and you'll get a nice reward. But be a brat and I'll leave you locked up all night." He reached behind her with the key and unlocked her handcuffs from the pole.

Alexa immediately sprang to her feet, her schoolgirl skirt flouncing up around her smooth thighs. Her eyes blazed with rage. She was spitting mad, but her words were choked out by the gag still in her mouth. Stefan watched her cautiously. "Are you going to be a

247

good girl?" he asked.

Alexa breathed heavily though her nose. She maintained her stare, but it gradually softened as Stefan held her gaze. He was winning their silent standoff. And eventually, she let her eyes drop down. She gave a simple nod.

Stefan reached for the gag. "Good girl," he said, slipping the rubber ball from her mouth.

Alexa stretched her jaw angrily, rubbing her cheeks to feel the blood come back. Her nostrils flared. "You son of a-"

Stefan cut her off with a sharply raised hand. "Quiet, kitten," he ordered in that calm, firm voice. He kept Alexa's eyes trained on his hand like a conductor. "Are you going to be a good girl?" he asked.

Alexa nodded. "Yes, daddy."

"Good," said Stefan. He stroked her cheek gently, brushing her tangled hair from her cheek. Then he beckoned her over to me. "Come."

Stefan raised his eyebrow at Emily. "Think your boy deserves a little reward?"

Emily grinned over at me. "I'd say so," she said. She unbuckled the leather strapon belt and let it fall to the floor.

"Got that key handy?"

Emily reached into her dress and rooted around inside her bra, finally pulling out the small gold key to my chastity cage.

"Good," said Stefan. He looked between Emily and Alexa. "Now, I want you girls to go give our friend here a nice little reward. So I want both of you on your knees."

The girls obediently knelt down between my legs. I looked down, scarcely able to believe the sight. Two incredibly sexy girls. One, my sweet loving girlfriend, looking up at me with caring eyes. The other, an incredible little minx in a schoolgirl outfit, her face smug yet alluring.

Emily grasped my chastity again, her hand wrapped all the way around my cock and balls. "It's so heavy," she said. "You must be dying for it."

"Look how tiny it is," Alexa smirked. "You really let him fuck you with that thing?"

"It gets bigger," said Emily. "You'll see." She looked up at me with soft but teasing eyes and that mischievous smirk. "Are you ready for your release?"

"Yes," I panted. "Please."

She rubbed the outside of the cage, and my desperation to feel that sensation was overwhelming. "Well, since you asked nicely," she said. Then she slipped the key into the small padlock and clicked it open.

Emily gingerly slipped the cage from my cock and placed the ring on the ground. Blood immediately raced into my member, washing over me with relief. "Look at that," Emily cooed. "It's waking up again."

She held my cock out, angling it toward Alexa. Alexa shot me a dirty look, then dutifully took my cock in her mouth. The feeling of her lips and tongue closing over my tortured member was exquisite. I immediately started swelling in her mouth, my cock unfurling itself.

Alexa sucked me under Emily's watchful gaze, until Emily pulled me from Alexa's mouth and took her into her own. She made happy gobbling noises as she worked my cock inside her mouth, sucking me down as deep as she could go.

It was like all my fantasies had come true. Two girls working on my cock together, taking turns sucking me, stroking me, even kissing my shaft up and down together. They kissed up to my tip, and then they kissed each other, their mouths meeting and their tongues working together. Emily kept my cock pinched in her hand as she kissed Alexa deeply, the two of them entwined as they knelt on the floor.

As they kissed, Emily began to slap my dick

against Alexa's cheek. She moaned at the feeling of my wet slaps on her, then broke off the kiss so she could take me back inside her mouth. I could tell that beneath her bratty persona she really was a cock-craving whore, just like my girlfriend. She devoured me hungrily, sucking me down as Emily kissed and licked my heaving balls while pressing hard against the base of the buttplug, driving it against my prostate.

Just a few minutes of this was too much for me. I'd spent so much of my day in agonizing frustration, hanging on the brink of orgasm, that it took only a little stimulation once my cock had fully revived itself. "Oh, my god," I groaned. "I'm close. I think I'm going to-"

Emily aimed my cock at Alexa's face, and Alexa obediently opened her mouth and let her tongue fall out. The orgasm surged up in me, more powerful than anything I'd ever experienced in my life before. My mind went blank. I nearly fainted. It was an out-of-body experience, my consciousness enveloped by a white wall of pure ecstatic bliss.

My first rope of cum splattered across Alexa's lips

and tongue. Emily then pointed my cock at herself, allowing me to drench her face with my next shot. She alternated back and forth between them, making me hose them down with the largest load I'd ever shot in my life. By the end, both girls were giggling with shock and surprise at the sheer volume of cum I'd sprayed all over them. Their cheeks and lips and tongues all dripped with my love, and they immediately set to work kissing and licking my load off each other. This sight was the perfect coda to all my frustrated denial. I felt like I was floating. I'd never been so happy before in my life.

When they finished cleaning each other up, Stefan stepped forward. He reached down, gripped Alexa firmly beneath her arms, and heaved her up over his shoulder once again. "Good pet," he told her, giving her an appreciative pat on her ripe bottom.

"Are you going to take care of me now, Daddy?" she whined. "You promised!"

"Of course, kitten," Stefan told her. He turned to us, Alexa cradled over his shoulder, and reached out his hand. "It was a pleasure meeting you both," he told us, shaking our hands in turn. "Thank you for such an enjoyable evening. If you are ever back in the area, please feel free to stop by my club any time."

We each thanked him for the evening, slightly stunned by what had just happened. We were both disheveled, dirty, and in varying states of undress, and yet Stefan spoke to us as if everything was perfectly normal. "Feel free to take a rest on any of the couches here, if you require," he told us, gesturing to the large, comfortable looking sofas in his office.

"Daddy!" Alexa whined.

Stefan flashed an apologetic smile. "If you'll excuse me," he said, patting Alexa on her rump. "I have some business to take care of." And he disappeared from the room, carrying Alexa over his shoulder. The last we saw was her feet kicking happily down the hallway before Stefan shut the door. And then Emily and I were alone together.

XII

We drowsed a couple hours on one of Stefan's oversized couches in the office, Emily cradled up in my arms. It took only moments for us to fall asleep; we were exhausted from all the day's many exciting turns. The thought that we had spent that morning in bed in our cabin, or that we'd seen Shining Rock mere hours before, was shocking to us. It felt like weeks had passed.

When we woke, we found our clothes. I found the pink panties where they'd fallen from my mouth onto the floor while Emily pounded me with the strapon. I showed them to her with a chuckle. But when I moved to put them on, she stopped me. "Hold on," she said. "You're missing something."

The chastity device, of course. She slid it carefully back up over my aching cock and locked it tight again. I had a feeling it would be a while until it was free again. The thought sent a shiver of excitement down my spine as I slid the pink panties back up my waist before locating my jeans.

The club was still packed with revelers as we made our way toward the exit. I wondered if they ever went to

255

sleep. We took our coats from the coat check, still staffed by the same mute man, and exited the club.

To our shock, the sun was starting to peek up over the mountains. A grey dawn spread over the chilly, windswept Asheville streets. I pulled Emily close to me to protect her from the gusting wind as we retraced our steps back through the streets.

We were mostly quiet on the drive back up the mountains. The rosy-fingered dawn spread out across the hills, lighting up the fall colors with a warmth that spread like joy. We felt that warmth inside us too, bumping along the roads with our fingers intertwined. I couldn't believe all the events of the past weekend.

I looked over at Emily to make sure she was still real. She was real, alright, curled up in the passenger's seat fast asleep. My heart overflowed with my love for her, and my incredible grateful disbelief that I'd managed to find someone as exciting and sexy as her, and that she wanted to be with me too. I squeezed her hand, and she made a happy murmur in her sleep.

When we finally reached our cabin in the mountains, it was all we could manage to drag our sleep-deprived bodies out of the car and into the cozy little house. We headed straight to the bedroom, stripped off our clothes, threw the heavy blankets over ourselves, and fell asleep in each others' arms.

ABOUT THE AUTHOR

I've used erotica to explore my sexuality ever since puberty. Back then, when I had fantasies about something I thought was wrong, I'd write it down as a story and hide it under my pillow. Eventually I'd get scared my parents would find the story, so I'd tear it into pieces and flush it down the toilet.

As an adult, I still enjoy writing down my dirty fantasies. But now, I share them on the internet with strangers. It's been an incredibly fun and rewarding experience. I also write non-porny stories, and I hope to start publishing works under my own name this year.

I'm a bisexual guy in a relationship with a wonderful woman. She has been incredibly accepting of my sexuality, and has encouraged me to share these stories with the wider world. I am so grateful to have her in my life. I used to feel so much shame and guilt about my fantasies and fixations, but learning to accept myself has been so freeing. I urge anyone who feels negativity surrounding their sexuality to open up and start being honest about how you feel- first with yourself, then with others you trust. It makes life so much less lonely.

If you enjoyed this work, please check out my other works posted on KDP. And please subscribe to my blog! I will update it when I publish a new story or offer a new deal on Amazon, and I'll try to include details about my writing process or other thoughts about my projects that a reader might enjoy.

BLOG: https://lewiscraneerotica.blogspot.com/

Also, feel free to email me. I love hearing from people who enjoyed my stories.

EMAIL: lewiscraneerotica@gmail.com

MORE STORIES BY
LEWIS CRANE

ZENIT

Ilya, a poor, simple student living in Saint Petersburg, falls into debt with the Russian mafia. As punishment, he is forced to dress as a girl and seduce Jorge Costa, a superstar soccer player, as part of a scheme to blackmail the soccer star into staying in Russia. But when a bond deeper than sex forms between Ilya and Jorge Costa, Ilya must decide if he will stay true to his secret task, or risk everything for love. A romantic thriller with tons of sex.

[M/M, Sissy, Crossdressing, Feminization, BDSM, Group Sex, Anal Sex, Humiliation] [104 pages]

ABBY'S PET

Bratty Abby knows her step-brother has a crush on her. She uses this to her advantage by turning him into her little submissive pet. What starts off as foot massages turns into a depraved domination that includes helping Abby service her insatiable boyfriend.

[M/F, M/M, M/M/F, Femdom, Sissy, Humiliation, Feminization, Cuckolding, Interracial Sex, Anal Sex, Oral Sex, Crossdressing, Foot Fetish, Step-Sister][28 pages]

THE PERSIA RENDEZVOUS

Tenderfoot soldier Levi gets sent on his first real mission: rescuing the beautiful diplomat Ada Lessing from a prison in Iran. But when he winds up captured, it is Ada who does the rescuing after revealing her

260

identity as a secret agent. She leads Levi on a daring escape for their lives while being relentlessly pursued by the evil Commander Haddad. Along the way, Ada must find new ways to protect their identity, including dressing Levi in a hijab.

[M/F, M/M, Vanilla, Pegging, Femdom, Crossdressing, Cuckolding, Group Sex][79 pages]

MISTRESS KLEIN'S FEMDOM GYM

Sophia Klein takes your gym training into her own hands, pushing you past your limits with teasing, denial, and lots of punishment.

[M/F, Femdom, Bondage, Punishment, Denial, Teasing][36 pages]

SNATCH COMPETITION

Carmen and Jo always push each other to the limit at the gym. But when Jo loses a wager to Carmen, she finds herself forced to do the hardest thing she's ever had to do- get all dolled up and be Carmen's wedding date. A sexy short erotic story for fans of working out, bad ass girls, and the highly underrated fantasy of forced tomboy feminization.

[F/F, Lesbian, Lesdom, BDSM, Tomboy, Humiliation][35 pages]

THREE IN A BARN

Klara meets Taras every Sunday for a romp in the hay during their sweet summer in Ukraine. One day, Taras brings his inexperienced, virginal comrade Ilya and asks Klara let him watch. But Klara has other ideas about how to teach Ilya the ways of love.

[M/M/F, Threesome][17 pages]

Printed in Great Britain
by Amazon

49305547R10148